SEPTIMUS
AND THE SPY RING

SEPTIMUS
AND THE
SPY RING

————◦◦◦————

STEPHEN CHANCE

·A BOOK FOR· ·NEW ADULTS· na

THE BODLEY HEAD
LONDON SYDNEY
TORONTO

British Library Cataloguing
in Publication Data
Chance, Stephen
Septimus and the spy ring.
(Books for new adults)
I. Title   II. Series
823'.9'1F   PZ7.C3592
ISBN 0-370-30189-7

© Stephen Chance 1979
Printed in Great Britain for
The Bodley Head Ltd
9 Bow Street, London, WC2E 7AL
by Redwood Burn Ltd,
Trowbridge & Esher
Set in Monotype Baskerville
by Gloucester Typesetting Co. Ltd.
First published 1979

CONTENTS

I

Chemistry

Captain Septimus Treloar strolled slowly across Westminster Bridge enjoying the soft May morning. London was at its best in the spring, and it was good to be back again—even in wartime London, and even if he did feel like something out of a musical comedy in his army officer's uniform. A kilted sergeant snapped him off a smart salute, and he hastily returned it, consciously having to remember to use the army rather than the police salute. In peacetime he was a policeman, an inspector in the CID, and London was his patch; but the war had swept him up and for the last eighteen months he had been nominally an army officer, but practically many other things. He had just returned from an investigation in Alexandria. He shivered, remembering the heat of Africa, remembering the man who would now undoubtedly be shot as a spy; a nice man, an Italian from Naples with a wife and family who had only been serving his country. Still, Admiral Cunningham's Mediterranean Fleet would be better for his absence. Even so, Septimus preferred crime to war. At least villains were villains and not patriots.

The offices in Storey's Gate were remarkable only for their almost total anonymity. A door leading straight off the pavement between a tobacconist's and a corset shop; beside the door a brass plate—which clearly had not been polished since 1939—proclaimed: 'Peabody, Rafferty, Peabody and

Slocombe. Solicitors'. Above it was a temporary notice painted on wood: 'RE Rail Transport Div.'

There were two flights of stairs covered with worn linoleum, then a battered door bearing the polite instruction 'Please Knock and Enter'. Miss Parsons, as always, was sitting at her army-issue desk, fingers on the keys of her typewriter. She was an elderly spinster with iron-grey hair and a face like a starving horse. Kind-hearted, ruthlessly efficient and totally humourless; like the Victorian cane hatstand, she was left over from Peabody and Co. Septimus was very fond of her.

'Morning, Mavis,' he said, hanging cap and gasmask on the hatstand, 'the boss is expecting me.'

'Good morning, Captain Treloar. I hope you had a pleasant trip?' It was as if he had been on an outing to Margate with a pack of cubs. Septimus had a sudden conviction that Miss Parsons had been sitting at her desk since he flew out to Alexandria.

'Yes,' he said, 'I sent you a dirty postcard, and the Sphinx, cash on delivery. Hope you got them?'

She looked at him over the top of her spectacles.

'No,' she replied. 'I expect the mail ship was sunk. Sir John is at the moment engaged with a gentleman from the Ministry.'

'Coffee?' asked Septimus.

'Not until eleven,' she replied severely. 'But you might try Sergeant Dickinson. He was boiling water five minutes ago. He said it was for a new explosive.' She started to clatter at the typewriter as Septimus went through the inner door.

He went into the workshop; it was a big room, cluttered with benches and machinery, and—surprisingly—commanding a wide view of the west front of the Abbey. Sergeant Dickinson was stooping over a gas ring in the corner.

'Morning, Hugh,' said Septimus, 'Can I have some of that hell brew?'

Dickinson looked up. His army uniform was ill-fitting and

8

his haircut far longer than regulation. He was a ballistics expert.

'Septimus! Welcome home, sir. Just in time for coffee.'

Septimus removed the parts of a Thomson sub-machine-gun and sat on the bench, drinking coffee and chatting.

'Thanks for dealing with that bullet so quickly,' he said.

'No trouble,' Dickinson replied. 'It took a bit longer than usual because it had flattened on the armour plate.' Characteristically he did not think of saying that he had worked non-stop for fifteen hours on the problem Septimus had set him. 'Of course you were right—it was a Luger. Who was he?'

'Civilian cook in Cunningham's kitchen,' Septimus said, and changed the subject.

Miss Parsons put her head round the door. 'Sir John will see you now, Captain Treloar.'

Sir John Masterton, Septimus's boss, sat behind his desk and blew down his pipe, engulfing himself in a cloud of smoke. Septimus thought of Moses on the mountain.

Sir John was not really a super spy, although war had brought him the responsibility of a large counter-intelligence organization. He was in fact a Cambridge don, a historian, bringing to his present task the incisive mind of a scholar. He suspected himself of being too personally involved with his staff: brave young men and women who could all speak at least one European language perfectly; young army officers and ex-detectives, like Septimus. He cared for them, and it hurt when they disappeared. He said some nice things about Septimus's recent assignment—omitting the fact that he had recommended him for a decoration. The authorities were not keen on decorations for spies—it made the writing of the citation so difficult. What could you say in the *Gazette* about a shoot-out in the cellar of an Alexandrian brothel?

He turned to a more immediate practical problem.

'I was sorry to hear about your flat, Septimus,' he said.

9

Septimus nodded. There really was nothing to say. On the previous day he had disembarked, stiff and sleepy, from the Halifax bomber and had slept throughout the train journey to Victoria.

The taxi driver had been unusually friendly as they had surveyed the gaping hole in Stimpson Street, Putney, where Septimus's flat had once been. Well . . . at least he wasn't married. He had stood, looking at the pile of bricks, noting the remains of his wardrobe, feeling curiously free. He now owned himself, the uniform he stood up in, and the contents of his suitcase.

Sir John was saying, '. . . so I booked you in. I hope you will find it comfortable.'

'Thank you, sir,' said Septimus. He would have to find out from Mavis what arrangements Sir John had made.

'Of course you're really due for some leave—overdue come to that. But an urgent job has just turned up and I've no one else to put on it.'

There were many possible answers to that, but Septimus merely said, 'Yes?'

'Good,' said Sir John. 'Have you ever heard of H2S?'

'H2S?' Septimus rummaged through his half-remembered school chemistry and came up with an answer. 'Stink bombs? Sulphuretted Hydrogen?'

The boss was relighting his pipe. 'Precisely. Actually it is a code name. An academic joke by an eminent scientist. H2S is a highly secret development of Radio Direction Finding which, as you know, helped the RAF to win the Battle of Britain.'

'That's the business of bouncing radio waves off an approaching aircraft so you can tell its range?' Septimus asked.

'Exactly. Now apparently, if you send the signal from the aircraft to the earth, the strength of the return signal varies with the terrain. It is therefore possible for a bomber to see a moving map of the land beneath the aircraft, despite blackout, and even in thick cloud. That is H2S.'

Septimus considered the significance of this. Because of the nature of his job, he was in possession of all sorts of highly secret information. He knew what the general public did not know: that despite the courage of aircrews, half the aircraft of Bomber Command never even found their targets, and of those who did, few dropped their bombs within five miles of the target.

'Useful toy for the RAF,' he said.

'Precisely. Now listen to this.' Sir John went to a cabinet in the corner, an affair like a gramophone. He lifted the lid and did something with the controls. Septimus realized that it was one of the new tape-recorders which were just coming into service.

'Germany calling! Germany calling!' He recognized the harsh voice immediately. It was Lord Haw-Haw, the renegade Englishman who broadcast regularly on behalf of the Nazis. He listened carefully. There was some gloating information about the success of the U-boat campaign, then a highly coloured account of what was happening in North Africa.

'Now. This is the bit,' said Sir John.

The scratchy recording continued: 'And Mr Churchill's Royal Air Force may hope to profit from its new weapons. But we know all about sulph . . .' The voice stopped abruptly, and there was only the hum of the recorder. Sir John switched off the machine and came back to his desk.

'The gap in the transmission lasts nine seconds,' he said. 'When it starts again Haw-Haw is talking about President Roosevelt.'

'So they shot one down,' said Septimus.

Sir John shook his head. 'It isn't in service yet. One *has* been shot down. The RAF were experimenting over Brest. The plane—code name O for Orange—went down in the Channel. There was one survivor: the rear-gunner, Flight-Sergeant Hamish Stewart. You'll have to go and see him— he's in hospital. Then there's this.' Sir John passed a tiny scrap of paper across the desk. It was a cigarette paper. Septimus looked at the coded message: an incomprehensible jumble of figures and letters.

'Well?' he asked.

'It says, "They have the details of H2S." It came from one of our people in Dublin.'

'Is that all?'

'Yes. The agent has subsequently disappeared.'

Septimus sat silent. It was better not to know any further details—even if Sir John would tell him. Because Eire was neutral and because of the comparatively open border with the North, Dublin was a hotbed of spying activity. He wondered momentarily about the agent who had 'subsequently disappeared' and had a sudden mental picture of Sir John saying to someone else, 'Treloar subsequently disappeared.' He turned away from the dark speculation.

'Any particular significance in Dublin?' he asked. 'Apart from the fact that it's crawling with Teutons.'

Sir John tapped out his pipe. 'Yes. The Navy have been experimenting with a development of H2S. They call it O4. And that is another academic joke. Apparently O4 is even better than H2S. The sailors want it for searching out U-boats. They've got an experimental flight at a place called Maydown—that's near Londonderry, just east of the border.'

Septimus exploded. He was tired and strained and not in the mood to suffer fools gladly. 'If we win this war it'll be a bloody miracle! Highly secret equipment, an air station five minutes' walk from an open border, and a collection of Paddys who are still fighting Cromwell. Why don't they just send the damn thing to Hitler in a Red Cross parcel and have done with it? Save a lot of time.'

Sir John smiled at him. He was fond of the big policeman. 'The thought had occurred to me. But the Navy have their reasons. They can try it out over convoys in the Western Approaches, and they're out of reach of most of the Luftwaffe.'

'They could just as well use Scotland,' said Septimus sourly.

'Precisely. But we cannot re-organize the Admiralty. Anyway Septimus, here's the file.' Sir John passed a bulky folder across the desk. 'You can stay here and read it. There's the air gunner. There are the scientists at Malvern who invented the contraption. And there's Maydown. It's Maydown for my money, but if they've got H2S, it's up to us to make sure they don't get O4.'

Twenty minutes later Miss Parsons went into Sir John's office with a cup of coffee for Septimus, Sir John having gone off to a meeting. She was a little shocked to see that Septimus was sitting with his feet on Sir John's desk. He was deep in the top secret file and merely grunted at her.

When she returned to the office just before lunch, Septimus and the file had vanished: the former by one of the other exits from the block; the latter back into the filing cabinet.

Septimus was sitting on the Embankment watching the barges plunge under Westminster Bridge, although the scene did not really register on his brain. H2S and bombers over Germany. O4 and aircraft over convoys in the Western Approaches. Lord Haw-Haw. A piece of paper. A dead counter-intelligence agent. He shivered, remembering John Donne's lines: 'Ask not for whom the bell tolls—it tolls for thee.' Flight-Sergeant Hamish Stewart in hospital in Bedfordshire. Egg-headed boffins in the classrooms of Malvern College. Well, he would start with Sergeant Stewart. Then Malvern. Then Maydown. He would have to work out his cover with the boss.

He was suddenly aware that it had started to rain. He got up from the seat and picked up his gasmask and hand luggage. He realized, to his annoyance, that he had forgotten to ask Mavis about the arrangements Sir John had made for him.

2

Safe as Houses

'Before the ending of the day,
Creator of the world we pray
That with Thy wonted favour Thou
Would'st be our guard and keeper now.'

At the back of the tiny chapel which had once been a stable
Septimus stood and listened to the Franciscans singing the
hymn from the office of compline. They did not sing it very
well. The last time he had been in the friary down by St
Katharine's Docks there had been twenty of them. Now
there was only a handful—the war had claimed the young
ones.

Compline ended and the friars filed out. Septimus remained for a while kneeling at the back, looking at the simple
chapel: the altar made from a manger; the hay rack left in
the corner; the lamp flickering above the Sacrament. 'This is
my body . . . this is my blood.' War and broken bodies and
bloodshed. He thought of the Italian awaiting the firing
squad and tried to pray for him against the sounds of closing
time coming through the boarded up windows from the Bull
across the street, but the words would not come. 'Pray for us
sinners, now and at the hour of our death.'

Father Dennis was waiting for him in the corridor.

'Septimus, come and have a cup of coffee,' he whispered.

Septimus's impish sense of humour got the better of him.

'But father,' he whispered back, 'what about the Greater Silence?'

Father Dennis was nearly as big as, and even uglier than Septimus. He had the battered face of a professional boxer— which he had once been, and he was as bald as a boxing glove. He raised the skin where his eyebrows would have been had he had any. Septimus giggled. The expression meant so exactly, 'Don't be such a bloody fool.'

The friar's cell was virtually indistinguishable from a prison cell. Dennis sat on the truckle bed, Septimus on the one upright chair.

'Septimus, it's good to see you.'

'And you. How's the Youth Club?'

Dennis handed him a cup of coffee. 'You know a bomb hit it?' Septimus had seen the hole where the hut had once been. It was the Youth Club that had brought them together. Together they had raised the money for the building, and together they had taught judo and boxing to youngsters in the East End. The two old friends talked for a while, then the priest looked at his watch.

'Come on, Septimus,' he said. 'Time for my Underground trip.'

They walked through the blacked out streets which Septimus knew so well: mean little houses, their doors opening straight on to the pavement. Now windows were boarded up, and there were gaps like missing teeth in the rows and piles of rubble everywhere. Septimus felt both sadness and anger for a place and people he had come to love. As they paced down the empty street, Dennis spoke:

'Septimus, you look tired under all that tan. Can you tell me about it?'

Septimus knew it would be safe. 'No,' he said, 'I can't. But you might pray for someone.'

'Who?'

'An Italian called Alberto. He's probably going to be shot next week and he's got a wife and kids.'

'I'll do that,' said Dennis, and fell silent. Monks and friars, Septimus reflected, understood the value of silence.

They plunged down into the tube station where bunks had been built all along the platforms and East End families were camped out. Father Dennis talked to all of them, and some of them knew Septimus and welcomed him, so that it was not at all like being in an air-raid shelter. It was like coming home.

'That's all right, Septimus. You need not apologize. Miss Parsons can cancel the hotel, and I am sure you were more comfortable with your Franciscan friends.' Sir John Masterton looked benignly at his erring agent. Remembering the appalling truckle bed, Septimus doubted the word 'comfortable'. But certainly, he preferred the friary to a hotel in Lancaster Gate.

'Now about your cover at both Malvern and Maydown . . .' Sir John lit his pipe and Septimus couldn't help thinking of a smokescreen.

'I'd thought about that, sir. It would be best if I went as an army specialist in station security—checking up on their barbed wire and so on. I can't go as a civilian because I'd be too restricted. I can't pretend to be a naval officer, and I don't know anything about electronics.'

Sir John's pipe was roaring like a bonfire in a brisk breeze. He threw a couple of signal forms across the desk. 'My thoughts exactly. As you will see, you are now a member of a unit called Special Camp Security.' Septimus looked at the signals. They were to be sent to the Radio Direction Finding Establishment at Malvern and to the Royal Naval Air Station at Maydown in Northern Ireland. They announced his impending arrival to run a check on security arrangements.The eminent name from whom the signal originated made Septimus open his eyes.

'I seem to be working for a very high-powered organization,' he said.

Sir John smiled. 'I thought it as well to use his name. We do want you to be taken seriously.'

'Do any of them know what it's really about?' Septimus asked.

'Only the Director at Malvern and the Captain at Maydown.'

'I see,' said Septimus. 'And does this SCS really exist? I mean, might I run into one of them?'

Sir John blew down his pipe. 'It exists only in my imagination. SCS *c'est moi.*' Septimus was able to manage the French.

Sir John brought the interview to a close. 'Well there it is— and good luck. Miss Parsons has got your papers. Oh! And Sergeant Dickinson has a suitcase of his own devising that you might find useful.'

The RAF Hospital at Donisthorpe was like many temporary wartime hospitals: an old country house which had broken out in a rash of Nissen huts joined together by corrugated iron cloisters. It was as if Donisthorpe Hall had turned into an enormous spider and was spinning a web across the park. When Septimus arrived after a weary journey in a train bursting with service personnel, he found that he was expected, and because the warning of his coming had been sent by Sir John, he was awarded treatment far beyond that warranted by his captain's rank.

This did have its disadvantages, however. They had moved Hamish Stewart into a private ward pending Septimus's arrival, the result of which was to petrify the Sergeant, who seemed to think that he was about to be court martialled. It took Septimus a full ten minutes to pacify the young man. But he was good at that sort of thing, so by the time Hamish was bold enough to say 'Well sir? What did you want to know?' he had learned a great deal about Hamish's life: his newsagency business in Edinburgh and his pretty wife Fiona.

'The H2S set,' he said.

17

'Sir. I'm not to talk about that. It's top secret.' The Sergeant was obviously startled, suddenly unsure of himself again.

'Good for you,' said Septimus easily. 'I wouldn't expect you to. My job is just to make sure Jerry hasn't got hold of it.'

Hamish considered a moment. 'I don't think he could have, sir. The thing was there when we took off because I saw it. And Charlie, the navigator, was using it over Brest, because I could hear him on the intercom. And when we hit the sea . . . well . . . there wasn't enough time for anyone to get it out before Orange sank.'

'Tell me about the ditching,' said Septimus.

There was not much to tell because Stewart had been knocked unconscious when they hit the water. He had come round to find himself in the crew dinghy—Tom Donaldson, the gunner from the mid-upper turret had very bravely hauled him into it.

'He deserves a gong if anyone does, sir. Shouldn't be lying here if it wasn't for Tom. He said, "You lie there, Jamie, while I go back for the others." I wanted to tell him not to, sir. I could see Orange was going. But I couldn't speak, sir.'

So Tom Donaldson had returned to the sinking Lancaster, and had not come out again; and slowly the semi-conscious Stewart had been carried away by the current. He had been remarkably lucky to be picked up by a vigilant minesweeper.

Septimus thought about the Sergeant's story, concentrating only on the facts. It was no good getting excited about heroism. The main point was that the H2S in O for Orange had clearly not fallen into the hands of the enemy.

The cross country journey to Great Malvern was like stepping back into a leisurely, pre-war England. Septimus was the only person in uniform in the two dilapidated coaches which trundled along from one tiny station to the next behind a clanking old tank engine.

Septimus put his feet on the opposite seat and briefly considered the case. O for Orange could be written off. That left Maydown and Malvern, and only the future could tell which. He did not have enough material to work on, so he put the question out of his mind, took paper from his bag and settled down to write to Hamish Stewart's wife.

As was to be expected, there was no taxi to be found at Great Malvern station. He set off to walk up the steep streets of the little town perched on the side of the hills which rose so dramatically from the valley of the Severn. It seemed un-English. Apart from the granite of the buildings, it reminded him of Greek towns he had seen perched precariously above the blue waters of the Mediterranean. He passed through the medieval gateway of the priory and reached the Victorian Gothic frontage of the college which now housed the RDF Establishment since Churchill had insisted it be moved from its original, vulnerable home in Swanage.

Inside the main gate there was a temporary hut surrounded by sand bags where Septimus presented his credentials to a sergeant in the RAF Police.

'That's right, sir. Squadron-Leader Burroughs said to expect you.'

Sam Burroughs! Septimus's best friend and closest police colleague. They had lost touch over the last year, but Septimus had heard that Sam was now involved in RAF security. If it was indeed Sam, Septimus's task would be greatly simplified.

The RAF policeman put down the telephone. 'He'll be along in a minute, sir. Now if you'd just sign here . . .' Septimus did so and was given a temporary pass. 'You give that up when you go out, sir. And collect it when you come back in.' Septimus nodded. Superficially the gate security was adequate—as you would expect with Sam in charge. You could not actually wheel out an H2S set on a barrow without someone noticing.

Despite the air force uniform he recognized Sam

19

Burroughs by his swift, gangling stride as he came round the corner by the school chapel. The meeting was fun. It was good to see one another again, and they extracted some amusement at the sight of their unaccustomed uniforms.

'Masquerading as an air force officer!' said Septimus.

'Well, you look like something out of an army pantomime chorus, Septic. Come on, I'll show you to your room.' Sam led the way down the steep slope from the main gate and along the edge of the wired-off playing fields to a hideous Gothic building which had evidently been one of the boys' houses before the school was ejected.

They went up the stairs to the first floor and Septimus watched while Sam produced a key to a door of massive Victorian proportions. It had brass fittings, including an embossed cover for the keyhole. It was quite a large room with a wide view over the playing fields.

'Come down to my room when you're ready,' said Sam. 'I'm just below you. We'll go across to my office.' He showed Septimus where the bathroom was and clattered down the stairs.

A quarter of an hour later Septimus was sitting in an armchair in Sam's office: a queer mixture between a police office —filing cabinets, telephones and clipboards—and a peculiarly inconvenient Victorian classroom with the blackboard still on the wall.

Sam leaned back and put his feet on his desk. 'Well, Septimus, what's it about, old son? Don't try and come that silly signal with me. You looking at barbed wire like a pregnant cow and investigating whether the kitchen maids are having it off with the boffins!'

Septimus told him exactly why he was there—he had no worries about security where Sam was concerned.

Sam whistled and ran his hands through his close-cropped black hair, and Septimus could see the grim expression on his bony face. He felt a surge of sympathy. If the leak was from Malvern it was Sam's responsibility.

'Who else knows about this leak?'

'Our people,' Septimus replied, 'and your Director, and the RN Captain at Maydown.'

Sam nodded. 'I've fixed for you to see the Director in the morning.' He got up and walked nervously about the office. 'Dammit, Septimus, I don't see how it could be from here.'

'Why not?' asked Septimus brutally. 'That security fence of yours wouldn't keep out a drunken vagrant after the Communion wine in the chapel. What's to stop one of your scientists carrying out the plans in his pocket? I bet you don't search 'em.'

A grin lightened Sam's worried face. 'Septic, if we did that, they'd all resign, go back to their universities and get on with some real work. Anyway, it's not like that. It's not a bloody weapons establishment—half a dozen blueprints of the latest piece of hardware stuck up the knickers of an ATS corporal.'

'Security's security,' said Septimus. He knew he was being unhelpful, but he could spare no one—not even Sam.

'Not here it isn't,' Sam replied with some violence. 'Here security's—people.'

'What do you mean?'

Sam continued his pacing. 'I've been here since they moved from Swanage. When I got the job I had all the usual ideas—spot checks, searches, and all the rest. I even had a few bright ideas of my own. When I put them to the Old Man, he said what I've just said to you—"If you do that they'll all go back to their universities." I nearly resigned on the spot. Glad I didn't, because after a bit I saw the Old Man was right.'

'So what do you do?' Septimus asked.

'We keep everything in watertight compartments. We've got six of the best scientific brains in the country working here. Each of them runs a section, none of them knows what the others are doing, and in each section only the boffin in charge understands the whole project.'

Septimus considered this. 'But there must be plans—calculations and things . . .'

Sam grinned. 'Easy to see you've never worked with boffins, Septic old son. Sure, there are plans and calculations. But they all have their own way of working. Half the calculations are on the backs of envelopes and the rest are in their heads.'

'But there must be drawings!' said Septimus.

Sam agreed. 'In the end there are working drawings, and we keep them very snug in the safe in the Director's office.'

'And who holds the keys?'

Sam did not answer the question directly. 'The safe has a combination as well as a standard lock, Septimus. One of the ideas that I did persuade the Director to accept—in case one of his scientists left the complete plans for the latest secret weapon on a train. Only the Director and the Deputy know the combination; and only one of the section heads and myself have keys.'

'So two of you have to be present to get the safe open? It must be damned inconvenient.'

'It is. And the boffins hate my guts for it—but it's safe.'

'Can the plans be taken out of the office?'

'They have to be. They're working drawings. But two people have to come for them and take them back, and they're used in workshops with not less than six people in them. I wouldn't say it was impossible to get photographs—but it would take a professional to do it.'

Septimus was silent for a moment. Mentally he took his hat off to Sam. He seemed to have made things as secure as possible, beyond keeping the plans permanently in the safe.

Sam looked at his watch. 'Twenty minutes to dinner. Fancy a noggin before we eat?'

The mess proved to be a large, temporary building on the edge of the playing fields. It was a large dining-room with a bar at one end. Sam collected drinks and they sat in a corner continuing their discussion.

'Six sections,' said Septimus. 'That means seven boffins including the Director who would know enough to give away H_2S.'

'That's right,' Sam agreed. 'Professor Beauchamp runs one himself.'

'Who's he?'

'Beauchamp? He's the Deputy Director. He did the work on H_2S I fancy.'

'So it must be one of those seven,' said Septimus tentatively.

For the first time Sam displayed real irritation.

'Oh, come off it, Septimus. They've all got long and distinguished careers. Three of them have been Cambridge dons for twenty years, one was Head of Physics at Leeds University, another's been Ferranti's chief designer since 1925. They're just a collection of brilliant scientists—middle-aged or elderly. Do you think they've been selling secrets to Adolf? Do you think I haven't checked? You can see the files in the morning if you like.'

Septimus was tired and hungry, but he managed to control his irritation. 'All I know is, Sam, that Adolf knows about H_2S. And that's what I'm here to find out about.'

Sam was still angry. 'Well, it wasn't from this establishment. You'd better go and have a look at Maydown.'

Septimus choked down an angry reply, realizing that he was tired and Sam was rattled to have his professional competence called into question.

'I'll do that, Sam,' he said, 'but there's time to buy you another drink before I sail.'

When he returned with the drinks Sam pointed with his cigarette: 'If you're going to Maydown,' he said, 'you'd better have a word with him.' There was a thickset RNVR commander standing at the bar talking to an RNVR sub-lieutenant in naval battledress. They looked oddly out of place among the civilians and RAF officers round the bar. The junior officer was young: hardly more than a boy. The

23

commander had grizzled hair, a scar across his cheek and two rows of medals on his chest.

'That,' said Sam, 'is Rory McLusky, CO of 707 squadron —that's the experimental unit at Maydown. The young gentleman beside him is Peter Swann, his Air Engineer Officer. Don't be taken in by his childish looks. He's a very fine engineer, so I'm told.'

'What are they doing here?' Septimus asked.

'They often fly over. We've an airfield a few miles away. They come over to pick up things and to ask questions about the equipment they're testing.'

'I'd like to meet them,' said Septimus.

'After dinner,' Sam replied.

But it did not work out like that. Commander McLusky finished his drink and looked comprehensively round the mess. Then he said in a loud voice, 'Let the dead bury their dead. Come on Peter, my lad, let's go and paint Malvern red.' He marched out of the mess with the little engineer bobbing in the rear like a rowing boat in tow.

They dined with the Deputy Director, and Septimus found himself totally out of his depth in a discussion about *Piers Plowman*. After dinner he excused himself as soon as he decently could and went through the gathering darkness to his room. He was very tired.

3

Things that Go Bump in the Night

Septimus stood in front of the heavy Victorian door of his
room and fished in his pocket for the key which Sam had
given him. He was about to put it in the lock when he paused.
Suddenly he was no longer tired and his policeman's instincts
were fully alert. He stood before the door, remembering how
it had been when Sam had unlocked it, and when he had
locked it himself before going downstairs. On both occasions
the brass cover for the keyhole had swung back into place. He
remembered the word 'pendulum' going through his mind.
But now the brass cover was stuck like the minute hand of a
clock at ten to twelve. He stood a moment, checking his
memory. The caution ingrained by years of police work was
reinforced by the desperate dangers of the last few months.
He knelt before the door, taking the pencil torch from his
pocket, shining it into the keyhole. There was no obstruction.
Cautiously . . . cautiously . . . he put the key into the lock.
Nothing happened. He rotated the key very carefully, sitting
beside the door now, his back to the wall. Nothing happened.
He turned the knob gently and inched the door open. It
creaked slightly, but there was no resistance. When the gap
was wide enough he slipped inside, moving quickly away from
the light on the landing.

There was no sign of movement in the room. He stood still,
his back to the wall for a full two minutes. Nothing happened.
He turned on the pencil torch and examined the switch by

the door. It seemed perfectly normal. He shone the torch all round the door, paying particular attention to the hinges. There was nothing out of place. Still using the torch he examined the light in the middle of the room, the table lamp, the lamp plug, and the fifteen-amp socket. There was nothing. He switched on the light. All was as he had left it in the room: the innocent looking case which he had collected from Sergeant Dickinson in the Storey's Gate workshop was still sitting in the middle of the chest of drawers. He opened the case and looked at the contents: nothing seemed to have been disturbed. Behind the left-hand lock there was a little flap in the lining, invisible to the naked eye. He turned it down and looked at the tiny revolution counter, which indicated how many times the case had been opened. It was reading 6 and it should have been reading 5. The case had been opened—so much for Sam's security. He emptied the contents of the case and opened the false bottom. All the varied tools of his trade were still there in neat compartments; however, he had no means of telling whether the false bottom had been discovered. Certainly, anyone who picked the case up empty would realize that there was something peculiar about it—it was far too heavy.

He stood a moment, considering. Since he had taken his document case with him when he went to Sam's office, there had been nothing in the room to indicate why he had come to Malvern. It was just possible that the intruder would come again. He took wire, a battery and a buzzer no bigger than his thumbnail from the case and set about rigging up a temporary burglar alarm. He fixed the battery in circuit with the buzzer, which he put under his pillow. He took the two free ends of the wire and taped one to the door handle and one to the frame, so that if the handle were turned the ends of the wires would come into contact and sound the alarm. He tested it three times, making sure it worked; then, satisfied, he locked the door and went to bed.

It was three o'clock when the buzzer woke him. He slid soundlessly out of bed and went to the open window. It was dark outside, the moon obscured by heavy cloud. He climbed out on to the fire escape and flitted noiselessly down the iron steps to the lawn which was cold and damp to his bare feet. He ran silently round the side of the house. The front door was ajar. He crept inside and stood motionless, listening. There was no sound coming from the blackness of the staircase. He considered waking Sam Burroughs, but put the idea aside. Sam slept lightly, but to go into his room now would leave the bottom of the staircase unguarded. So he waited, conscious of the rough doormat under his bare feet and of the cold night air swirling through the open door, chilling him through his thin pyjamas. He was a fool not to have put on a sweater. So he waited.

There came the merest rustle of movement from the blackness of the stairs, followed by a creak from the old boards. The noise stopped and there was absolute stillness again. It was as if Septimus could hear the thump of his own pulse like the stroke of an engine, and as if the intruder in the darkness was straining his ears to catch the measured sound.

Suddenly a torch beam stabbed out, white in the blackness above, taking Septimus by surprise. Even as he realized that he had miscalculated, the attack came, swooping out of the blackness, the torch beam swinging up like a searchlight, ready for the blow which Septimus knew must come. His reaction was swift, instinctive, born of his highly trained reflexes. At the last possible second he stepped sideways so that the blow aimed with the heavy torch grazed harmlessly down his arm. Blinded as he was, he twisted round and grappled with his opponent; he could feel cloth in his fumbling hands, then an arm which he began to twist and tried to force into a half-nelson. The man was not as heavy as Septimus, but he was wiry and strong. He kicked back at Septimus, catching him painfully on the knee so that he stumbled, losing his grip on the arm. The intruder ran back up the stairs. Septimus, half crouching, saw him as a vague silhouette against the flickering, glancing light of the torch.

The running stopped, and the torch beam steadied, swinging down on to Septimus, illuminating him like a stage spotlight. Guessing what was going to happen, he did the only thing he could—threw himself sideways. Even as he did so, he was aware of a flash of red fire beside the torch, a sudden pain in his shoulder, and the strangled 'phut' of a silenced automatic. He rolled over on to his hands and knees. He could hear footsteps running frantically away from him and the torch went jerking and bouncing upward, throwing shadows in a crazy kaleidoscope of black and white. The fire escape! He stumbled to his feet, feeling his left shoulder with his right hand. Blood was running over his fingers, but he judged that it was only a flesh wound—at least he was still able to use his arm. As he started up the staircase, the torch was switched off. He was cursing himself. He had not expected that shot out of the darkness—and he should have done. Alexandria was one thing, but it was hard to believe that you would be shot at in a boys' school in England.

He reached the first landing and paused. The footsteps were still climbing ahead of him. He ran on and up, swift and catlike. Below him he heard Sam Burroughs's door open, and as he reached the second landing Commander McLusky came out of his room wearing purple pyjamas, light spilling from behind him on to the linoleum.

'What's up?'

'Intruder,' snapped Septimus, hardly pausing, 'Get Burroughs—cover the back door and the fire escape.'

He paused at the next landing, horribly conscious of the light below and the gun in the darkness above. He could hear three voices below; McLusky had probably routed out the sub-lieutenant engineer. The more the merrier—for there must be several ways out of a boys' boarding house.

From above came a muffled sound, a cross between a scrape and a rumble; somebody was opening a heavy sash window. Septimus took the final flight of stairs in three bounds and paused, crouching against the wall away from the light. It must be the room to the right because that was the side of the fire escape. Flat against the wall, he eased the door open and then dived in, hurling himself across the room away from the opening, the speed and power of his lunge taking him to the far wall. The room was empty, the window open, its frame an oblong silhouette against the cloud-obscured moon, the curtains swaying gently in the night breeze. He peered cautiously out of the window. There was no one on the fire escape gallery and no sound of anyone descending. There was movement below on the lawn and the white blob of an upturned face.

'That you, Sam?' he shouted.

'Yes,' Sam called back.

'Seen anything?'

'No.'

'Well stay there in case he doubles back.'

Septimus went along the fire escape gallery to the corner and peered carefully round. There was a dark figure about ten feet away, next to a window; he was facing inward, the white blur of his face half turned toward the corner. Septimus saw the intruder's arm come up and swiftly drew back his head. Three sounds mingled into one: the firing of the silenced gun, the whine of the bullet passing the corner, and the sound of breaking glass. Septimus strained his ears, listening for the sound of the window being opened—that would be the moment to charge; but no sound came, and after a while he took another look round the corner. There was no sign of the man down the whole length of the gallery. Septimus guessed that the window had refused to open so that there was only one place for the intruder to go—upwards, on to the roof. At the end of the gallery there was a steel ladder fixed to the wall, and without pause Septimus went up it, climbing as fast as possible in case the intruder was waiting for him at the top. But there was no one. Beyond the parapet the slate roof climbed steeply, with a lead-lined gutter between its bottom edge and the parapet. There was no sign of the intruder along the dark perspectives of the roof, only a forest of chimney pots and sewer vents dimly outlined against the sky. He must have gone along the gutter and round the end of the gable, seeking another way down from the roof. Immediately in front of Septimus was a ladder lying flat against the tiles and leading up the steep slope of the roof —evidently he had chanced on the school building department's inspection route.

The wooden ladder was not an easy climb for someone with bare feet. There was room for little more than his toes, and the square angle of the rungs cut into his flesh; but he turned his toes outward, painfully made his way up to the ridge, and looked over into the valley beyond. To his right it was closed off by a stretch of roof connecting one gable to the other; but in the open 'V' to the left he could see the shadowy figure of the man he was following.

He watched in silence, aware of the gun, only the top of his head and his eyes above the ridge. The intruder switched on his torch, and by its light Septimus could see another ladder leading from the valley to the connecting ridge between the two gables. He ducked as the beam of the torch came sweeping toward him along the ridge.

He waited a moment, then looked over again. The valley was dark now, but to his right he could see the intruder making his way up the connecting ridge, a darker shadow in the darkness, bulky on the ladder, like an enormous spider. Hastily Septimus clambered over the ridge and descended into the valley, moving as fast as he could, feeling naked and vulnerable; fearful of the stab of white torch light and the muffled explosion of the gun. He slid the last few feet and ran, stooping low to the foot of the ladder which the intruder was still climbing. Without pause he hauled it away from the slates and started to drag it along between the two gables. He could feel the top end sliding on the slates; he could feel the timber of the uprights bending under the strain. There was a cracking noise and one of the uprights broke—it had not been designed for such treatment. There was a cry from above, and suddenly the ladder came free so that Septimus stumbled and fell with the ladder half on top of him. He extricated himself and looked up. The intruder was clear against the dark sky, sitting astride the ridge facing Septimus. Septimus turned and ran for his life, but the bullet between the shoulder blades did not arrive. He flung himself round the gable end and stood trembling between the face of the gable and the parapet. There was a slithering noise from round the corner, a scream and a crash . . . and then silence.

Septimus closed his eyes. 'Dear God,' he thought, 'there was no parapet at the back.'

When Septimus got down from the roof, he found Sam with a group of other people standing round the body of a young man dressed in slacks, gym shoes and a dark roll-neck sweater. Sam was obviously pleased to see Septimus still in one piece, but was too occupied with the immediate problems to say much. Like Septimus, he realized that the last thing they wanted was publicity.

'Septimus!' he said. 'Glad to see you. Looks as if you've distinguished yourself by catching our camp thief.'

'Camp thief?' Septimus asked, willing to be led by Sam.

'Yes. We've had a lot of pilfering over the last few months. Knew it must be somebody who lived inside the wire, but we've never managed to catch him.'

'Who is he?' Septimus asked.

'Chap called Reggie Fieldman. Clerk in the general office.'

One of the policemen suggested that they ought to get a doctor, but Sam brushed the idea aside since Fieldman was obviously dead.

'A matter for the civilian police,' he said. 'And there's nothing much they can do. Put him on the sofa in my room.'

When they had done so Sam sent his RAF policemen back

to the guardroom with strict instructions to keep their mouths shut.

'If you men talk,' he said, 'we shall have God knows what rumours of spies flying around the place.' The police went, leaving Commander McLusky and Peter Swann. The Commander grinned at Sam. 'Sneak thief? First time I ever heard of a sneak thief pooping off with a silenced gun!'

'That's one of the things we've got to find out about,' said Sam, 'so I'd be obliged if you'd both keep your mouths shut too.'

Half an hour later, Sam Burroughs was leaning over the body which lay on the sofa in his sitting-room talking to Septimus as he turned out Fieldman's pockets. He had strapped up the wound in Septimus's shoulder, which had proved to be a mere nick in the flesh above the collar bone, and the two men had returned to Sam's rooms to discuss the incident.

'So you see, Septic, you needn't have indulged in heroics all over the roof. When McLusky woke me I turned out the emergency squad. Had the place surrounded in two minutes flat.'

Septimus sighed and put down his glass of whisky. 'So I shan't get a medal after all,' he said, stirring in his chair to ease his aching shoulder. Sam pulled the blanket back over the body and came across to the gas fire.

'Find anything?' Septimus asked.

'Not a thing. I should think he changed into that gear specially to come and burgle you.'

'How did he know I was worth burgling?'

Sam shrugged. 'Damned if I know, Septic. Probably just guessed. Knew there'd be a barney about H_2S and wanted to find out if you were part of it. After all, you were billed as "security".'

'Sam, you'll have to keep it under wraps. Can't have the locals detecting all over the place.'

'Ooh, I think I can do that. I know the local Chief, and if

the worst comes to the worst I'll wave the Official Secrets act at him.'

'What about those two naval officers?' Septimus asked.

'Oh, they're all right. They're pretty security conscious at Maydown. Piggins—their Security Officer—is a good bloke. I'll have a word with them in the morning. Threaten to get them drafted to the Far East if they breathe a word.'

'Which leaves defunct Reggie,' said Septimus. 'Sam, do you think Reggie was the man I'm looking for?'

'Couldn't possibly be. General office? He wouldn't know anything worth leaking. But he is—was—obviously the contact this end. No, Maydown's the place.'

'What puzzles me,' said Septimus, 'is why did he take a shot at me? Gave me no end of a turn that did. I wasn't expecting it.'

'He panicked,' Sam replied. 'You've seen it yourself, Septimus—a villain surprised on the job. Now they've got firearms, that's the only difference.'

Septimus thought for a while, then replied slowly: 'I think it was more than that. Reggie knew his stuff. He got out of my half-nelson like a commando instructor, and he didn't go for the door after he missed me with the torch. He knew he hadn't got time. No, I think he carried that gun because he was afraid I was very important—and a threat. And if he was prepared to kill . . . it probably means they are very close to something big. And that probably means O4.'

Sam continued the train of thought. 'He wanted to know if you were really just checking up on me, or after him. And if you were, he'd probably have killed you anyway.'

Septimus nodded. 'Sam,' he said, 'can we do his rooms before the camp comes to life?'

Sam looked at his watch. 'It's a quarter to four,' he said. 'We've just about time if we get a move on.'

4

Communications with Ireland

Dawn was lightening in the east, over the line of the Cotswolds beyond the Severn as they walked along the edge of the playing fields to Fieldman's quarters. They walked in silence.

Septimus was sickened by the memory of Fieldman sliding from the roof; his screams would be engraved on his memory for ever. He was seized with an inexpressible longing to be done with this 'cloak and dagger' business, this ruthless life of kill or be killed. He couldn't stop thinking about Sam and himself drinking whisky with a blanket-covered corpse on the sofa . . . the brutalization of war. He found himself longing to be back in the CID dealing with honest crime. Honest crime! He smiled at the phrase. In the meantime he had a job to do.

Fieldman's quarters were on the edge of the playing field, down past the pavilion. They consisted of half a Nissen hut. In the centre of the concrete floor was a round coke stove. Sam took off the top and poured in more coke, then they looked round the ugly, functional cabin.

The furniture was basic service issue, made of varnished softwood: a table, a couple of chairs, one armchair, a desk under the window, a wardrobe, a chest of drawers, and an iron bedstead made up with grey service blankets. The only individual items of furniture were a large bookcase on the partition wall, and on the table a record player and a powerful radio.

'I'll start with the desk,' said Septimus. 'You do his clothes.'

They worked for an hour, mostly in silence, and then Septimus eased himself into the armchair, wincing at the pain in his shoulder. Sam drew up an upright chair, opened the bottom of the stove and gave it a violent poke, setting the flames roaring up the cast iron pipe.

'Impressions?' Septimus asked.

'So normal as to be highly suspicious,' Sam replied. 'He's lived in this room for more than six months, and it's as bare of personal touches as a hotel room. About the only thing that tells you anything about the man is that pile of *Belfast Advertisers* in the corner. And all they tell you is that he's interested in Belfast—because he worked there once. And I knew that already.'

Septimus agreed. 'There's not a single personal paper in his desk—apart from a few local bills.'

'Wallet contained four pounds ten shillings,' said Sam, 'driving licence, identity card, establishment pass, photo of a girl called Shelagh, and a love letter signed by a young lady of the same name.'

'Let us be charitable,' said Septimus, 'and assume that it's the same young lady.' He took the photograph, looking hard at it, fixing the features in his mind, conscious that Sam had already done the same thing.

'Any other suspicious items?' Septimus asked.

Sam snorted. 'A series of Baedeker Guides in the bookcase; the German ones much used in 1937 and 1938, annotated in pencil with names and dates.'

'He was interested in Rhine castles,' said Septimus.

Sam sniffed. 'You needn't tell me. A powerful radio tuned to Berlin, and a taste in classical music leaning heavily toward Wagner—just like Adolf.'

'And just like a few hundred thousand Englishmen,' said Septimus. 'It doesn't add up to a row of beans, Sam.'

'No. The only really suspicious thing is that there's nothing —not even a dirty book. That adds up to a dead cert.' Sam picked up the letter. 'In fact the only personal thing we've got is this.'

The address was 5 Limavady Court, Londonderry, and the letter was dated three days previously. It was signed 'Your darling Shelagh', and had Septimus been that sort of man, he would have blushed to read the catalogue of endearments which it contained. Among the 'longings' and the 'love' and the vows of eternal loyalty, there was really only one concrete fact. Apparently Fieldman had sent a parcel to 'Shelagh', and there had been a customs query about its contents.

She wrote: 'I was sorry, darling, to hear that there had been trouble about the parcel. You do not say what sort of trouble. It could hardly have been the police kicking up a fuss since it was only half a pound of sugar! Don't tell me that the customs people are all that interested!'

Septimus let the letter drop into his lap and leaned back, deep in thought. Was it illegal to give away your sugar ration? Not so far as he knew. And did Customs investigate the mail between England and Northern Ireland? He doubted it. There were no tariff barriers between two parts of the United Kingdom.

Sam broke in on his train of thought. 'Code, Septimus?'

'I doubt it. At least, if it is, it's a very simple one. Sam . . . do you censor outgoing mail?'

'No point, old son. They can always post a letter in the town.'

'What do you do about the internal mail?'

'There are half a dozen boxes about the place. It goes into a mailbag and the GPO collect it each morning. You thinking about that queer reference to a bag of sugar?'

'Yes, I was,' said Septimus. 'You wouldn't need a code—only thirty or forty agreed symbols. Suppose H_2S was the chemical symbol for sugar?' He heaved himself, wincing, out of the armchair. 'Let's go and have a look at that mailbag. It's just possible that Reggie has replied to this letter.'

He had. They left the sergeant in the guardroom to put the

mail back in the sack and went in triumph to Sam's room bearing the letter addressed to Miss Shelagh Hurst in Limavady Court in Londonderry.

'Miss Shelagh Hurst,' said Septimus, weighing the letter in his hand. 'I think, Sam, we should deal with Reggie's love life as it deserves.'

Sam filled the electric kettle and plugged it in, calling over his shoulder, 'You think it'll explode like an IRA bomb, Septimus?'

'You know damn well what I mean,' said Septimus without rancour.

While the kettle was coming to the boil they subjected the envelope to a minute scrutiny under the bright light of Sam's desk lamp. It revealed nothing. Once the kettle had boiled, Sam slipped a rubber nozzle over the spout so that the steam came out in a thin jet which they applied to the flap of the envelope. Septimus gently coaxed the flap open with a kitchen knife, laid the open envelope on Sam's blotting paper and carefully extracted the folded sheet of notepaper. Cautiously he unfolded the letter, holding it by the corners and bending them flat on to the blotting paper. He looked down at the open sheet and grinned. 'Oh Sam! What it is to be suspicious!' he said. With finger and thumb he carefully extracted a single human hair from the fold in the notepaper.

Sam grinned in response. 'Virtue is its own reward,' he said.

The letter itself was so like the one from 'Shelagh', with its banal protestations of affection, that it might have been written by the same hand. There was a little more factual information about Fieldman's way of life: he had been for a walk on the hills, he had been to the cinema. There was also a reference to the parcel: 'Do not worry about the parcel, darling. I'm in touch with the authorities and should soon know all about it. A lot of damned nonsense! Anyway, you've eaten the sugar by now, so they can't do much about it. I'll let you know as soon as it's all cleared up. Meantime don't worry your pretty head.'

37

'You could be right, Septimus,' Sam said.

Septimus was carefully replacing the hair and putting the letter back in its envelope. 'You'll have to deal with that,' he said, jerking his head in the direction of the still shape under the grey blanket, 'I'm leaving this end to you, Sam. I want to see Miss Shelagh Hurst before she hears about lover boy. How do I get to Maydown?'

'Larne—Stranraer boat train,' said Sam. 'Or the Navy fly a DH86 from Liverpool. Or I tell you what, McLusky and Swann will be flying back today. Cadge a lift with them.'

So they parted; Sam to return the letter to the mailbag and deal with the local police, Septimus to snatch a couple of hours' sleep.

Septimus was later for breakfast than he had intended. He had found dressing and shaving difficult because of his shoulder. He stood in the doorway and looked round the room with its sprinkling of silent civilians and RAF personnel. There was no sign of McLusky, but Peter Swann was sitting alone at a table by one of the windows. Septimus collected his food on a tray and went across to him.

'Mind if I join you?'

The young man looked up with a quick and friendly smile. 'Be my guest,' he said. Then, as Septimus was transferring his food on to the table, he asked, 'How's the shoulder, sir?'

'Feels as if the rats have been at it,' Septimus replied.

'What was all that about last night, sir?'

'You heard what the man said. We caught the camp thief.'

Swann looked at him. 'Armed with a service .38?'

Septimus put down his spoon. 'Look, young man, this place is highly secret. So if things go bump in the night, you keep your mouth shut if you want to stay out of trouble.'

Swann was unrepentant. 'I can see my wavy stripe blowing in the breeze,' he replied. 'But really, sir, we do take security seriously. Rory's very hot on it.'

'Tell me about him,' said Septimus.

'He's quite a boy is Rory. He's Irish, mad as a hatter and I should think about the best pilot in the Air Arm.'

'Why isn't he with an operational squadron?' Septimus asked.

'Too old, I suppose. Won his DSO in 1917. Spent the inter-war years in civil aviation. He ran a mail line in Australia, and the first commercial line in Peru. Barnstorming, trick flying, racing—you name it, Rory's done it.'

'And what about you?' Septimus asked.

'Oh, I'd just finished at London University. Mechanical Engineering. So now I mend aeroplanes when the pilots bend them.'

'You mean you try to mend them, you nasty little plumber.' It was Commander McLusky himself, and neither of the other two had noticed his approach. He sat down and scowled at Septimus, creasing the scar on his face. 'I've just had words with that oppo of yours, the flat-footed copper dressed up like a Brylcreem boy. Talking to me about security. I told him what he could do with his truncheon. People pooping off .38s in the middle of the night . . .' He paused and pointed to the dubious yellow concoction on his plate. 'And what's this?'

'Scrambled egg, sir,' said Swann. 'Reconstituted variety. Kind permission of our American allies.'

McLusky snorted. 'Looks more like the lining of a self-sealing petrol tank . . . tastes like it as well.' He glanced at Septimus. 'And what are you going to do today? Health-giving walk on the hills?'

'I was hoping,' said Septimus, 'to cadge a lift from you to Maydown.'

'Coming to gaze at our barbed wire, are you? Glad to— co-operation between the services and all that.'

After breakfast Septimus went to take his leave of Sam. There was a bespectacled clerk standing outside the office who presented him with a note.

Dear Septimus,

    I have the local inspector with me. You have gone to N. Ireland. Keep out of the way. I'll look after this end. Be in touch.

                        Sam.

The small airfield that served the scientific establishment was about six miles away in the flat valley of the Severn. There was no runway, a couple of small hangars and a single all-purpose hut. It was a morning of fitful cloud and sunshine with a sharp wind blowing out of the north. To the west the long line of the Malvern Hills dominated the horizon like some enormous sea monster inexplicably stranded on dry land.

The three men went into the crew room where the naval officers donned their flying kit. They managed with some difficulty to find a helmet large enough for Septimus, and Rory McLusky loaned him a scarf of vast length.

'Dublin University Rugger Fifteen,' he said. 'I should hate to see you actually freeze to death.'

Swann slid a parachute pack across. 'Know how to fix it and use it?' he asked. There was a hint of malice in the question. The Senior Service demonstrating its superiority to the stupid soldiery.

Septimus merely nodded, resisting the urge to point out that he had already jumped out of two aeroplanes—which was no doubt more than Swann had done.

They clumped out to the waiting aircraft, their parachutes bumping against their hams.

The aircraft was a Swordfish, Rory McLusky's own, and known affectionately as 'Gertie'. Septimus viewed it with a certain speculative reserve. He had sampled a good many RAF aircraft over the last two years; but at least they were metal-clad monoplanes. This thing was an ungainly fabric-covered biplane with two open cockpits and a fixed undercarriage. It looked like something left over from the First World War. Directed by Swann, who showed him where to put his feet so that he did not poke holes in the fuselage, Septimus clambered awkwardly into the observer's seat in the rear cockpit. He strapped himself in, and after some difficulty found where to plug in his intercom. There was a spurt of blue smoke from the engine, the three-bladed propeller turned unwillingly a few times and then the engine roared into life. McLusky did his cockpit check and signed the serviceability form which a mechanic, his hair blowing in the slipstream, held up to him; then he waved the chocks away and they were trundling over the grass and turning into the wind.

'You all right back there?' McLusky's voice was tinny over the intercom.

'Yes,' he replied. McLusky waggled the stick a couple of times so that the aircraft shook its tail from side to side like a duck coming out of the water. He applied the brakes, brought the engine to full power so that the tail was almost lifting; then they were off, bumping over the grass, and then suddenly airborne.

Had it not been for the cold that numbed him, starting with his hands and feet and spreading inexorably to every part of his body, Septimus would have enjoyed the trip. They flew comparatively low—he guessed at about two thousand feet—droning slowly northward. He saw Worcester below him with the spring sunshine bright on the cathedral. He picked out the Wyre Forest as they passed west of the industrial haze over Birmingham. Half an hour later the high Peak District reared up to their right, and they swung westward, skirting Liverpool, and so out over the Irish Sea.

By this time Septimus was so cold that he had slumped down in the cockpit in a semi-sleep which was more like a coma. He was awakened by a thump on his back. He looked over the cockpit side and saw—much to his alarm—massive cliffs towering above them to the right. He turned left, and was even more alarmed to see another cliff nearly as formidable as the first. They were flying through a canyon, the aircraft bumping and lurching, and beneath them was the sea. He turned to look at Swann who laughed at the astonishment on his face. He scribbled a note on a signal pad and passed it to Septimus. 'The Isle of Man and the Calf. Rory doing his stunt pilot bit.' Septimus grinned wanly at him and settled himself once more for sleep. It seemed a very silly way to get killed, but there was nothing he could do about it. His coma re-asserted itself so that he did not see the approach of the soft greens and blues of Ireland with its scattering of cottages like specks of white paint on a green canvas. He was unaware of the smoky sprawl of Belfast, the dockyard cranes like praying mantises, or the shallow waters of Lough Neagh, and was only bumped into wakefulness by the turbulence as they climbed over the Sperrin Mountains with Londonderry already in sight ahead.

They came down over the gentle landscape where a light rain was falling and landed in time for a late lunch in the Maydown wardroom.

After lunch Septimus was eager to be off to Londonderry—though he told no one why.

'Can't do that, my lad,' said McLusky. 'Have to report to the Duty Officer. Old Man will want to see you. Tell you about the perimeter fence, I shouldn't wonder. Young Peter here will look after you.'

Septimus cursed inwardly. He was not interested in Captains RN. He wanted to investigate Shelagh Hurst. But with a policeman's patience he accepted the inevitable, thrust the investigation to the back of his mind and concentrated on Peter Swann's potted introduction to RNAS Maydown as they walked to the guardroom by the gate.

The station was simple enough, and almost exactly the same as hundreds of others. There were two massive corrugated-iron hangars facing one another across a wide expanse of tarmac: one for the anti-submarine squadron, one for Commander McLusky's experimental flight. For the rest, there was the usual huddle of Nissen huts and asbestos buildings to house personnel and provide offices and work-shops. It was a bleak and flat place running down to the shallow waters of Lough Foyle to the north, and to the south to a sizeable range of round-topped, inhospitable mountains.

'The mountains round here are quite high for this part of Ireland,' said Swann. 'The pilots don't like them because they're very wild, and if you do get into trouble there's nowhere to land: that is, unless you're Rory.'

'And what did the gallant Commander do?'

Swann laughed. 'He had an engine failure—fractured fuel pipe. So he put the Stringbag down on the one straight stretch of an unmade road and called us up on his radio. But it was getting dark and we didn't find him till dawn. There he was, sitting in the driver's seat, waving a pearl-handled Colt .45 in the middle of a slanging match with an Irish shepherd . . . shepherd and aircraft surrounded by about ten thousand sheep. I thought he'd be in a flaming temper, but he wasn't. He'd bought a stone jar of moonshine from a passing tramp and was three-parts plastered.'

'What did you do?' Septimus asked.

'Patched up the fuel line. Then Rory insisted on flying the thing home. Did a perfect take off as well.'

'Tell me about the experimental flight,' said Septimus.

'Nothing much to tell. We've got five Swordfish, Rory, three pilots, three observers, me and Jerry—he's the wireless wizard. We try out the boxes of tricks over Western Approaches for the Malvern boffins.'

'Do you enjoy it?' Septimus asked.

'Anyone who didn't enjoy working for Rory would have to be round the bend,' Swann replied with a smile and a charming simplicity which endeared him to Septimus.

Since Sam Burroughs had had the good sense to ring from Malvern, the officer of the watch was expecting Septimus, and welcomed him 'aboard'—a pleasant naval fiction which made Septimus smile. He told Septimus about his cabin and said he had to report to the Captain as soon as he had stowed his gear.

Captain McLeod, DSO, DFC, RN proved to be a wizened little man with practically no hair and a face like Mr Punch. He wore a uniform which fitted him perfectly and yet managed to give the impression that it was a size too large for him.

He greeted Septimus cordially and then came straight to the point.

'Officially Treloar, you've come to look at the perimeter wire. In fact it's because there's been a leak about H2S.'

'Yes, sir. We don't know where the leak happened. It could be Malvern, it could be here.'

McLeod picked up a ruler and held it between his palms, looking up at Septimus and frowning, shrewd grey eyes under bushy eyebrows.

'I think it's here,' he said.

'Why do you say that, sir?'

McLeod put down the ruler and leaned back in his chair.

'My Security Officer—name of Piggins—he's a good enough chap about sentries and passes and censorship and so on. But he can't cope with—and can't be expected to cope with—treason.' He paused on the dramatic word and then went on. 'We're too close to the border. Civilian employees and people constantly going ashore. We're not to be trusted with secret equipment, and Their Lordships ought not to let us have it.'

'But a security risk doesn't add up to treason,' said Septimus reasonably.

'It's not just us,' said McLeod. 'It's the dockyard and the convoy escorts. I want you to go and see the Port Admiral. He's very worried about sabotage, leaks and so on. You go and see him, Treloar.'

'I'll do that, sir.'

'Now. Piggins is expecting you.' The Captain grinned. 'I may say he's scared stiff. Thinks the Admiralty is after his

44

blood. Meantime, is there anything more I can do for you?'

'Transport, sir,' Septimus replied. 'I shall need to be able to get about.'

The Captain picked up the phone and asked for Motor Transport. He was connected, issued a few abrupt orders and put down the phone. It took about twenty seconds, then he said 'Go down to MT, they'll fix you up.' He stood and held out his hand. 'Keep me informed, Treloar.'

'Thank you, sir.' As Septimus took the proffered hand, he was already planning the future. 'Oh, and one other thing, sir—have you got a padre?'

The Captain looked astonished. 'A padre? Of course we've got a padre.'

'Is he a big man?'

McLeod looked even more astonished. 'No, he's a little fat man. Why do you ask?'

'Nothing, sir,' said Septimus absently, 'I was just thinking. I only hope he's fat enough.'

5

The Woman in the Yellow Scarf

As Septimus closed Captain McLeod's door a tall young RAF flight-lieutenant uncoiled himself like a spring from a chair in the outer office and advanced with outstretched hand.

'Captain Treloar?' he asked. 'I'm Piggins, the Security Officer.'

Septimus took the limp, bony hand in his own solid fist. An

irreverent rhyme floated into his mind—something to do with 'flipper' and 'kipper' . . . He would have to adjust his ideas, since when he had first heard the name Piggins it had conjured up a picture of someone with pink eyes and a curly tail: certainly not this pleasant beanpole of a young man with lank hair and a friendly smile.

Mr Piggins smoothed his blond hair with a nervous gesture. 'The officer of the watch told me you'd arrived and were with the Captain, so I came across straight away. If you'd care to come to my office, we can talk about the security of the camp.'

'Poor lad,' Septimus thought. 'He's scared stiff.'

'No,' he said, 'that'll keep. You know, Mr Piggins, no one's questioning your security. They just send me round trying to be helpful. It's a load of cobblers really—I always find naval security top-line. Wish I could say the same for the Army. What I really want is for you to lead me to your medical officer. Then I'll have a mosey around, and then we can have a chat. After I've seen the padre, that is.'

Flight-Lieutenant Piggins was so puzzled by this peculiar speech that he did not utter another word until Septimus had disappeared into the sick bay. He looked at the closed door and shook his head in wonder.

'Crackers,' he said. 'Clean round the bend.'

The medical officer was out so Septimus delivered himself into the hands of a cheerful sick berth attendant who removed Sam Burroughs's temporary dressing from Septimus's shoulder and viewed the wound with some concern.

'Nasty, sir. How did you get it?'

Septimus was deep in thought about Londonderry and Shelagh Hurst.

'Bullet wound,' he replied.

'A bullet, sir?' The SBA sounded puzzled. Septimus brought his mind back to the present with an effort.

'Yes. You know. Lead thing. You pull the trigger and it

comes out of the spout. Nasty dangerous things, guns. Do people a mischief. How fat is your chaplain?'

'Excuse me, sir. Are you feeling all right?' The SBA was wondering whether he had a case of delirium on his hands.

'Of course I'm all right. I asked how fat is your chaplain? Perfectly reasonable question. Not a parlour game like "How high is a Chinaman?" Well—how fat is he?' The SBA was hurting his shoulder, and Septimus was feeling irritable.

The SBA made a professional decision to humour this military nutcase.

'Well, sir,' he said, swabbing at the shoulder, 'he's fat-like.'

'Is his neck as far round as mine?' Septimus asked.

'Oh yes, sir, I should think so.'

'Good.' Septimus lapsed into deep thought about Londonderry, and the conversation came to an end.

As the SBA had said, the padre was indeed 'fat-like'. He was a friendly, cheerful little man called Bird, and in Septimus's opinion he ought to have swapped names with Piggins. Since he was wearing a cassock and there was a statue of the Blessed Virgin Mary on a shelf over his head, Septimus reckoned he was a high churchman and called him 'father'—no doubt it was a pleasant change from the everlasting 'padre' of the services. Since he had an odd request to make, Septimus set himself out to be pleasant. He found it an easy task because the tubby little priest was so warm-hearted. They discovered that they had various mutual friends among the Franciscans and that Bird's peacetime parish was next door to Septimus's peacetime 'patch'.

'Well,' said the priest at length, 'and what can I do for a neighbour?'

'An odd request, father,' Septimus replied. 'I want to borrow one of your clerical collars and the black bib thing that goes underneath.' Bird looked astonished, then he started to laugh so much that his rolls of fat shook.

47

'A dog collar and a stock! What on earth do you want them for?'

Septimus laughed in response. 'Well, I could tell you it was for an army concert, but you wouldn't believe me.' He pulled one of his several identity cards from his pocket and placed it on the desk. 'Security, father,' he said, all mirth gone from his face. 'I need to borrow them and I can't say more than that.'

There was a simple dignity in the priest's immediate seriousness.

'Of course. Come across to my cabin now.' He paused and an impish smile crossed his round face. 'What size collar do you take?'

The MT officer was a dour Scot who was very obviously in high dudgeon at having to lend one of his precious vehicles to an army officer. However Septimus thanked him politely and drove off in his newly acquired fifteen-hundredweight van to the control tower where he borrowed a large-scale map of the area. He gratefully accepted a large mug of tea from a cheerful blonde Wren and spent a profitable half-hour studying the lie of the land, noting particularly the proximity of the border. 'What a damned silly place to test secret equipment,' he muttered.

It was about six o'clock when the red and white painted pole at the entrance to the airfield lifted for Septimus and he turned on to the road to Londonderry. It took him some time and several enquiries to locate Limavady Court, but eventually he ran it to earth down by the docks, where the cranes towered over mean houses, grey in the incessant rain.

It was an alley between two warehouses. He stopped the van at the kerb, took a look up and down the cobbled street and hastily removed his khaki collar and tie, replacing them with the chaplain's stock and clerical collar.

'Church militant,' he muttered to himself as he walked down the alley.

The court was a small paved square surrounded by three-storey houses, number five being identical to all the others, except for a printed notice in the window which said 'Bed and Breakfast'. The jangling of an old-fashioned bell produced a small, old-fashioned woman with grey hair in a bun who proved to be the landlady.

No, she was very sorry, Miss Hurst was not at home. She was at work. Where did she work? She was a barmaid at the Royal George down by the Royal Dock. The gentleman couldn't miss it if he went to the end of the street, turned left and went as far as he could go.

Back in his van, Septimus sat for a few moments, considering. Was it best to storm the Royal George as a straightforward army officer or as a padre? The question really hinged on whether Shelagh Hurst had yet heard of Fieldman's death—which in turn depended on whether there were any other members of the ring in Malvern. He decided on balance to remain a parson, and could only hope that the Royal George was the sort of pub in which a padre would not look out of place.

When he drew up outside it, it confirmed his worst fears. It was a large, garish building of red brick with mock Tudor gables, totally out of sympathy with the grey stone buildings which surrounded it, and with the oily waters of the dock which faced it. He sat for a moment on a bollard, his back to the dock, contemplating the frontage of the building. In peacetime it had been lit with rows of electric bulbs. It must have been the very epitome of a sleazy gin palace. Now it was just sleazy and not at all the sort of place for a clergyman. He sighed and went in.

As he entered there was a sudden silence in the long bar with its round, marble-topped tables and sawdust-covered floor. It was not just surprise at this military-clerical apparition—it was plain hostility. He could feel it like something tangible in the air. He marched firmly to the bar, recognizing with a grim *frisson* his instincts about the place. It was the way a man felt when he was afraid of a knife in the back.

There were three people behind the bar: two women at the far end, and nearest to him a man with a drooping moustache which reminded Septimus of a Mexican bandit in a Hollywood Western.

'Miss Shelagh Hurst?' he said. 'I believe she works here.'

The bandit jerked his head. 'That's her with the red hair.'

'I wonder, landlord,' said Septimus, doing an obsequious imitation of a parson, 'I wonder if you have a room where I could talk to her privately? You see, I have some personal news for her—rather bad, I fear—which . . . really . . . I would prefer to communicate in private.'

The red-headed girl was looking at him down the length of the bar.

'There's an office down the corridor you can use, padre. I'll tell her.' As the landlord moved down the bar, two men got up from one of the tables and walked toward the redhead carrying empty pint mugs. It was an innocent enough move, but it made the warning lights flash in Septimus's brain. If two men were drinking at a table, only one of them normally went to get the mugs refilled.

The Mexican bandit came back. 'She'll come when she's finished serving those customers. I'll show you the office, mister.' He held up the bar flap and led Septimus through a curtain into the corridor. He opened a door, switched on the light and ushered Septimus into a little office. 'She won't be long,' he said, and closed the door.

Septimus looked round: there was a roll-top desk piled high with papers; a couple of chairs and a safe in the corner. The curtains were already drawn although it was not yet blackout time. Septimus went to the window and drew back the curtains. There was a yard with outhouses on two sides and a high wall with double gates on the third. He undid the catch of the window and cautiously slid up the bottom sash. Then he let the curtains fall back into place. He went to the

50

edge of the window frame and inched back the curtain so that he could see into the yard without being seen. Tense, he waited, his ears occupied with the sounds in the pub behind him. Footsteps in the corridor. Two pairs: a woman's and a man's. The man's stopped outside the door of the office, the woman's went softly on down the corridor. He heard the sound of a door opening, then the red-haired girl appeared in the yard. She was wearing a raincoat and a yellow head-scarf, and she was carrying a suitcase. She hurried to the big gates and let herself out of the yard. Septimus dropped the edge of the curtain and ran across the room, moving with an absence of noise astonishing in so big a man. He put his ear to the crack of the door. There was the merest scuffle of a foot on bare boards and a rustle of clothing. With great care, as soundlessly as possible, he moved the catch on the Yale lock and allowed the bolt to slide into place. Despite his care it made the slightest of clicks as it went home. There was a movement outside the door and the knob turned.

Septimus ran back across the office and climbed out of the window into the yard. He crossed the yard and let himself out of the gates. He found himself in a narrow cobbled lane which backed on to a row of small gardens. In the lane there was a little boy playing with a ball who watched in some astonishment as Septimus sprinted up the lane, round the corner and out into the street that ran along the quay. Lounging on the far side of the street were the two men he had seen in the bar. A hundred yards up the street the red-headed girl was walking quickly in the direction of the town. Septimus turned to follow her, aware of the loungers behind him. He walked swiftly and heard the clatter of footsteps behind him.

'Hey, mister!' one of the men was shouting. 'We want a word with you.' As Septimus turned he saw the girl start to run. He stood smiling at his two opponents.

'Yes?' he said in his best parsonical manner. 'I saw the young lady leave, so I followed. I have a message for her.

You're friends of hers I take it?' As he talked he was sizing up the two men. One short and broad—he would be heavy. One tall and thin—a long reach. 'Tweedledum and Tweedledee', he thought idiotically. They came toward him, slowly now, hands in pockets. Septimus stood easily, arms loose, casual, a smiling parson. The tall man smiled back at him. It was not a pleasant sight.

As always, in the timeless moment of action, Septimus was aware of many things: the last gleam of the setting sun on the oily water to his left; the lonely hoot of a warship in the river; the crying of the gulls. The big man drew his hand from his pocket. There was a gleam as of fire from the metal of the knuckleduster as he swung his right arm back. At the last possible second Septimus dropped on one knee and hit the tall man hard in the solar plexus. The tall man grunted and doubled up like a deckchair. The force of the blow made him spin round so that he was thrust between Septimus and the other attacker, who was brandishing a piece of lead pipe.

Using his bent leg as a spring, Septimus hurled his first assailant into the face of the smaller man. They both went down in a tangle of arms and legs, rolling and cursing across the cobbles. Septimus, now on his feet, assisted the rolling mass with a couple of swift kicks. The two men scrambled away from his swinging foot—as he knew they would. The smaller man—Tweedledum—struggled to his knees, the length of lead pipe still in his hand. Septimus stooped and hit him hard under the jaw so that he fell over backwards, the length of lead pipe rolling into the gutter. Septimus assisted the roll with his toe so that Tweedledum went over the edge of the quay. As he went he clutched at his companion. Together they hit the oily water with one loud splash.

Rubbing the knuckles of his right hand, Septimus looked down at them as they floundered toward the ladder on the side of the quay.

'I should have explained,' he said. 'I'm a Baptist minister, and I believe in total immersion.' He turned and ran for his van. It was facing in the wrong direction, but he did not bother to turn round and went roaring over the cobbles and round the corner at the end of the street.

A policeman was standing on the second corner of the block. Septimus stopped the van and leaned across the passenger seat.

'Oh, officer,' he said, 'as I passed the end of the quay just now, there were two men fighting outside a pub. I thought I ought to let you know.'

'Thank you, sir,' said the policeman. 'Soon sort them out.' He set off in the direction of the Royal George. A gentle grin stole across Septimus's homely features—it looked most unholy above the borrowed clerical collar. He sat for a moment with his hands on the wheel. He had already forgotten the minor fracas and was considering his next move.

The girl had clearly been warned from Malvern and was changing her base. But because of the lift with Rory McLusky Septimus had arrived at least twenty-four hours before he could reasonably have been expected. So who had warned her and how? Fieldman was dead, so there must be a second agent at Malvern. He would have to warn Sam about that. Of course there was another possibility—Rory McLusky or the little engineer. He smiled at the improbable idea.

And where was she going? Another base in Londonderry? That was hardly likely—the town was not big enough. To lose herself in Belfast, then? Septimus called to mind the map he had studied in the control tower. The main line and the bus station were in opposite directions. He thanked God for petrol rationing—wherever she was going, she would have to use public transport. That only left the narrow-gauge railway line . . . and that led over the border into Eire. He would lay a sizeable bet that that was where she was headed; out of the country by the first available train.

He let in the clutch, sorting out the basic geography of the town as he drove, working round in a circle to avoid the town centre and to reach the station before the girl. He took a couple of false turns, but reached the little station with about five minutes in hand before the girl could possibly arrive. He parked the van in a convenient cul-de-sac from which he could watch the station entrance, and ran across the road to the booking hall. He examined the timetable. There was only one more train that evening—and that was in forty minutes. He went back to the van to wait. Two minutes later the girl hurried into sight and went into the booking hall. Septimus watched her go up to the ticket window and fumble with her handbag. Then she disappeared on to the platform. He reckoned she was safe for the next forty minutes, and leaned back, considering his next move.

His objective had changed since the episode in the Royal George. Now the last thing he wanted was to see the girl— but he very much wanted to know where she was going and who she was going to meet at the other end. Yet in uniform he would be far too conspicuous. He cursed himself for his lack of foresight. He should have put civilian clothes in the van.

He was brought back to the immediate present by the measured tread of boots as an army patrol passed the end of the cul-de-sac. It wheeled across the road and went into the station. The army uniforms made him realize something he should have appreciated before, and he cursed, using language which was a disgrace to Chaplain Bird's collar. Not only would he be conspicuous in uniform, he could not even board the train! Or if he did, he would certainly get arrested as a belligerent in Eire. He had no desire to spend the rest of the war in a Free State prison. He looked at his watch. He had thirty-five minutes in which to find a civilian disguise. The shops were shut and there was no time to drive back to Maydown. Suddenly he chuckled. A parson he was and a parson he would remain! With plans forming in his mind he let in the clutch.

The Roman Catholic cathedral was only three minutes' drive away. He parked the van and consulted the gilt lettering on the black notice board. Benediction was safely over.

Confessions were being heard for the next half-hour. Well . . . at least the faithful would be sufficiently occupied with their own sins not to take too much notice of his.

He took off his cap, dipped his finger in the holy water stoup, crossed himself, murmured, 'Forgive me, Lord,' and went softly into the cathedral.

6

Over the Border

Inside the cathedral it was warm and dark and smelt of incense. The twilight came dull through the heavy stained glass, votive candles gleamed and flickered in front of brightly painted statues. There were a few people kneeling at the back of the nave and a whisper of speech came from one of the row of confessional boxes. A printed card proclaimed that Father Patrick was on duty. Septimus strolled slowly across the back of the nave, remembering to genuflect to the tabernacle on the high altar as he passed the central aisle. He went on down the far side, past the statues and the little chapels. He found the vestry door behind the pulpit: it was hidden from the nave, and he blessed his luck. He turned the handle softly. The door had been left open.

Septimus stepped inside, closed the door, locked it behind him and switched on the light. It was as most other vestries: an antiquated safe in one corner, a vesting chest under the window with printed prayers on the wall above it, a sink, and built-in cupboards. There were two other doors, an arched exterior one, and another which clearly connected with the living quarters of the cathedral clergy. The outer door was locked, the inner one standing ajar. Septimus opened it six inches and peered into an empty corridor. There was neither sound nor light. He extracted the key from the corridor side and closed and locked the door. He felt safer now, but knew he must hurry since time was slipping away. Swiftly he opened cupboards: albs, lace cottas, stoles; what appeared to be a Sunday School cupboard full of books, drawings and crayons; and—yes!—cassocks.

He put his hand to the bottom hem of the largest cassock and traced it up to the hook. He held it against his body, tried the sleeves against his arm. It would do. Thank God the cathedral had at least one large priest. But did RC priests go around in cassocks in a Protestant city like Londonderry? He was not sure. He paused, irresolute. His eyes rested on the blackout curtains at the window, and he almost laughed aloud. If only the vestry ran to a pair of scissors! He rummaged through the Sunday School cupboard, and found a pair among the pots of glue and boxes of paint.

He dumped cassock and scissors on the vesting chest, climbed up and unhooked one of the blackout curtains. Now he needed one more thing. He looked comprehensively round the vestry from his high perch. There was a chest in the far corner. He jumped down and opened it, disclosing vases, a broken statue of St Francis, a pile of disintegrating hymn books, and a tangle of thick ropes—some red and some white. More than he dared hope for! He hauled a length of white rope from the chest. It was about ten feet long and had a brass hook at either end. Evidently it was used for roping off parts of the cathedral. He made a bundle of the articles he was stealing, wrapping them in the blackout curtain. He took a last, quick look round the vestry, searching for further props for the part he had planned for himself. He added an office book and a rosary, dropping them into his pocket. On the back of the door there was a voluminous priest's cloak which would do much to hide the deficiencies of his disguise.

He took it, picked up his bundle, unlocked the door leading into the churchyard and was about to depart when he suddenly realized that he would need pins. But there were none —neither on the table, nor in the drawers. Then he spotted a stapler, seized it and dropped it into his pocket—that would serve his purpose better than pins. He picked up his bundle and made for the outside door. As he did so the handle of the church door turned and there was an exclamation of annoyance from the other side. Evidently Father Patrick had finished hearing confessions. Septimus ran out into the graveyard, locked the door behind him, threw the key into a corner and walked swiftly away in the soft twilight.

When he got back to the cul-de-sac he climbed into the back of the van and worked with frantic haste. There were barely thirteen minutes before the train was due to leave. He cut the tape and hooks from the top of the curtain, folded it lengthways and stapled the two edges together. Then he folded it the other way, cutting off the excess so that when doubled it would reach from his shoulders to halfway down his shins. Next he cut a neat semi-circle out of the folded end, making a hole large enough to go over his head. Finally he stapled the edges of the hole together. He took off his army tunic, transferring the contents of his pockets to the cassock, put on the cassock and his imitation monk's scapular. He cut the white rope to the right length, tied at one end the knots representing the three monastic vows of poverty, chastity and obedience, and fastened it round his waist. He put on the cloak, climbed down to the cobbles, and walked in what he hoped was a demure fashion towards the station. There were four minutes to spare before the train was due.

The first test of his new personality as a Benedictine monk was the military patrol which was having a 'stand easy' in the booking hall. Septimus, aware of his brown officer's shoes, was glad that the hall was ill-lit by a single inadequate oil lamp. The patrol sergeant saw him coming and called to his men: 'Now then! Look lively there. Make way for the padre.'

Septimus smiled benignly at him. 'Thank you, my son,' he said, and went up to the ticket window. He bought a third-class return to the last station on the line, and went on to the low platform.

The train was already waiting, and he walked along its length, rosary in hand, telling his beads and glancing into each compartment as he passed. The girl was sitting in the corner of a compartment at the back of the train, gazing white-faced out of the window. Septimus strolled slowly past, head down, intent on his beads, his lips moving. The first compartment in the last coach was empty, so Septimus climbed in and seated himself in the corner. He took out his stolen office book and laid it on the seat beside him, open at the office of compline.

Surprisingly the train started on time and they trundled through the blacked-out back streets of Londonderry and away westward into the coming night. They had hardly gathered speed—a full twenty miles an hour—when with a great jolting and grinding of brakes the little train drew into a wayside station and stopped with a portentous jolt and much hissing of steam. And at that moment the lights came on. Septimus turned to the window to pull down the blind when he realized that the platform was illuminated and the name-boards had not been removed as they had on all British stations. It was the border.

There was the tramp of official feet and the slamming of doors. Septimus could see the familiar uniforms of British military police and customs officials, and the unfamiliar ones of the Eire Customs. He draped his cloak half across his lap so that it hid his brown shoes, picked up his office book and started to mutter compline with as much conviction as he could muster—which was very little, since he did not know any Latin.

The door opened and he was aware of a khaki uniform on the edge of his field of vision. He finished mouthing an incomprehensible sentence and looked up with a benign smile.

'Good evening, my son,' he said to a craggy-looking military policeman.

'Evening padre, and sorry to disturb you.' The military policeman moved on down the train. The Eire Customs official who followed a few moments later did not even bother to open the door, simply contenting himself with glancing through the window.

With a waving of lanterns and blowing of whistles which would have graced a more modern means of transport, the little train lumbered into motion again until it was rattling along at its top speed of just over twenty-five miles an hour. Septimus settled back to enjoy the unaccustomed spectacle of the twilit countryside dotted with the soft glow of oil lamps in cottage windows. He dozed for a while, and was suddenly awoken by the squeal of brakes: they were clearly stopping again. He stuck his head out of the window. They were approaching a wayside halt, a low platform with a solitary white-painted hut in the centre of it. 'Killegaran.' The name-board on the fence was illuminated by the train lights. Septimus drew back and waited.

A solitary door slammed, and a moment later Septimus saw Shelagh Hurst moving away from the train towards the station exit. Swiftly he opened the door on the far side of the compartment and stepped down on to the track. As he did so, the whistle sounded and the train groaned into life. Ahead was a bridge carrying a road over the line and Septimus started to walk toward it, keeping pace with the train. As the train gathered speed, so he had to break into a clumsy trot, gathering the skirts of his cassock in one hand, the cloak thrown over his shoulder. He could not help laughing at himself. He must look a bloody fool, and surely St Benedict had never hurried? He reached the bridge and stood facing it as the rear of the train rattled past, its red tail lamp whisking out of sight like a conjuring trick, and the noise of its passing suddenly cut off by the bastion of the bridge.

Septimus was aware of silence as he waited to see which

way the woman had turned. A cow lowed somewhere in the field to his right, and was answered by the bray of a donkey from the huddle of lights—a farm perhaps, or a hamlet. He heard the swift clack of the woman's footsteps on the hard surface of the road and slipped silently beneath the arch of the bridge. The footsteps stopped over his head for some moments. Evidently Miss Hurst was a cautious young lady, making sure she had not been followed. He heard her move away, and as the footsteps faded he slipped from under the bridge and poked his head through a gap in the hedge. The narrow road ran straight for about a quarter of a mile to where the lights of the houses started. He moved swiftly, under the protection of the hedge, keeping behind the sound of the footsteps until his progress was cut off by a barbed wire fence. He laid his cloak over the wire, tucked his cassock into his girdle and vaulted lightly over. Unfortunately the corner in which he landed happened to be a favourite meeting place for cattle so that his feet slid from under him and he sat down in a mixture of mud and cow dung, and by the time he had extricated himself from this Irish morass he looked more like a cowman than a Benedictine monk. Because of the delay he had fallen behind, and the footsteps were very nearly out of earshot.

He ran, stumbling along the edge of the field, to the gate in the corner at the back of a range of outbuildings. There were half a dozen cottages of whitewash and thatch with a more substantial building on the far side of the road. There was a mangy dog rooting in a pile of rubbish, but no human being in sight.

Septimus climbed the gate and put on the cloak which fortunately had not suffered muddy disaster. He walked steadily through the hamlet, trying to look as if he belonged, aware that even a real Benedictine monk would cause comment in such a tiny community. Fortunately no one saw him except a ragged little girl in a cottage doorway who was sucking her thumb and watching him in silent wonder. 'God bless you, my child,' he said as he passed. She crossed herself and ran into the cottage to tell her mother about the strange 'father'.

The larger building proved to be a pub called the Red Cow, which, like the cottages, was whitewashed and thatched. Against the wall was a horse trough with a rail above it. Tied to the rail were two small donkeys with enormous packs on their backs, and a big black horse with a patch of white on one of its rear legs.

The pub stood at the crossroads and there was a signpost beneath an oil lamp on the wall. There was a main road running through the village, and crossing it was a mere cart track. There was no sign of Shelagh Hurst—she had either turned up one of the unmade roads or gone into the pub. Septimus walked round the end of the building and found a gate leading into a muddy yard with a midden in the centre and a pile of barrels by the back door. There was the sound of an animal rooting in the mud and a pig grunted at him, surveyed his cassock and then retreated behind the midden. Beyond the barrels there was a soft glow of light from the bar window. Swiftly Septimus crossed the yard, fearful lest the back door should open. Cautiously he rolled one of the barrels away from the wall so that he could crouch behind it beneath the window. No sooner was he hidden than the back door opened and a man crossed the yard. Peeping through the spyhole which the curve of the barrels allowed him, he saw the man disappear into an outhouse. He smiled in the darkness. All country pubs had urinals in the yard. He eased himself up and looked in at the window.

The ground floor of the Red Cow consisted of one room with an earth floor. There were a few rough tables with stools and barrels to sit on, and at the far end loft steps without bannisters led up to the first floor.

The girl was sitting half facing the window at a table in front of the peat fire which smouldered on a stone slab beneath a vast stone canopy. The canopy trapped perhaps half the peat smoke, leaving the rest to hang in a blue cloud beneath the low rafters. She had taken off her headscarf and was leaning forward in earnest conversation with a man whose back was to Septimus: a heavily built man, wearing a wide-brimmed tweed hat and a grey belted raincoat with epaulettes. Septimus's policeman's eye noted a small triangular tear on the left shoulder.

It was a frustrating situation. Septimus would have given a month's pay to be able to eavesdrop, but no matter how hard he strained, he could make nothing of the scarcely audible murmur which penetrated the window. All he could hope for was a sight of the unknown man's face. His ears picked up the sound of a car approaching. It drew closer, slowed down when it reached the hamlet and stopped outside the pub. The unknown man walked to the door. Well, at least Septimus would get a look at his face when he came back into the bar. But it was not to be. The back door opened with a crash and a man staggered rather than walked into the yard. He was clearly very drunk, and seemed to have some difficulty in remembering the direction of the gents. He crashed into the pile of barrels and started cursing in Irish. Septimus crouched low in his hiding place, waiting for the drunk to sort himself out. At last he reeled away and Septimus was able to turn to the window again, just in time to see Shelagh Hurst walking out of the door which was being held open for her by a tall blond man in a beautifully tailored overcoat, who looked Swedish but was much more likely German.

Septimus was about to leave his hiding place—was indeed halfway round the screen of barrels—when the back door was opened wide, sending a stream of yellow light which lit up the steaming midden. In the doorway a man—presumably the landlord—was struggling with an empty barrel. Septimus drew back into the shadows and waited for the banging and bumping to cease. It seemed to take a long time, and when it was finally over someone inside the bar complained loudly about 'the peat reek', so the landlord left the back door wide open, illuminating half the yard.

Septimus cursed and set off to make a wide detour round the midden only to find himself face to face with the drunk who was setting a course from the gents to the bar, and cheering the voyage with a bibulous rendering of a hymn to the Blessed Virgin Mary.

> 'May the Mother's intercessions
> On our homes a blessing win . . .'

He saw Septimus and the singing broke off abruptly.

'Holy Mother of God! It's the Divil himself. No, it isn't then, it's a father . . .' He put loving arms round Septimus's neck and rested his head on his shoulder. 'Father, will you hear my confession? I've been at the Guinness again.' He started to cry.

Septimus looked desperately over his shoulder at the open door, extricated his neck from the encircling arms and supported the drunk with one hand while he fumbled with the catch of the nearest outhouse door with the other.

'Yes, my son,' he said, 'I'll hear your confession. Come into the box.'

He swung open the door, pushed the drunk inside and closed the door again. As he ran from the yard the squeals and grunts and the shout of 'bloody pigs!' indicated only too well the nature of the outhouse.

He was too late. As he reached the corner of the pub the black horse was already disappearing towards the border and the big car was pulling away in the opposite direction. He was just in time to see the diplomatic plate on the back.

The noise behind the pub was getting much louder, and it sounded as if all the pigs had got out of the sty to join the one Septimus had encountered in the yard, and as if the clientele had left the bar to engage in a pig hunt. There was a patter of trotters and a pig came skidding and squealing round the corner, an Irishman in close pursuit. They ran off in the direction of Strabane. both too intent on the chase to take any notice of Septimus. It was, however, clearly time to depart.

Propped against the wall by the horse trough stood an elderly bicycle with an open wooden box fixed to the carrier. Septimus commandeered it, rolled up his cloak, dropped it into the box, and tucked up his cassock once again. He mounted and pedalled off in the direction of Londonderry. He was only just in time. There was a sudden eruption of pigs from the pub yard, and a voice shouted, 'The thievin' father's stolen me bike!' The pigs were abandoned in the excitement of the new chase, but all the advantages were with Septimus, and he soon left the pursuit behind.

He settled down to pedal steadily, reckoning it would not take too long to catch up with the horse, provided it was not ridden faster than a canter. After about ten minutes he heard the sound of hooves ahead. He rode a little closer, then settled down to maintain his distance behind the horseman. So they proceeded for a further twenty minutes until Septimus was beginning to wonder about the border and whether the horseman had a legitimate reason for crossing, when the rhythm of the hooves changed. Septimus came to a halt, listening. The rider was dismounting, leading the horse off the road. He heard a creak and a scraping noise and guessed that a gate was being opened. The horse whinnied, there was a scuffling sound and then silence. Septimus pedalled slowly on until he came to a gate which led to a lane between un-kempt hedges and overhanging trees.

There was no sound of the horse, so he opened the gate, wheeled the bicycle through and rode off up the dark lane. He quickly found that riding without lights on an unsurfaced Irish lane was a hazardous undertaking. He skidded once and nearly fell off, hit an unseen pothole and almost went over the handlebars, and finally rode into a sizeable and unseen boulder with such force that he buckled the front wheel and had to abandon the stolen bicycle.

Philosophically he set off on foot, thankful that the lane

was easy to follow. So he continued for an hour, climbing steadily—as Peter Swann had said, it was indeed wild country. Looking back he could see far below the huddle of lights which was the hamlet of Killegaran, but for the most part there was only darkness. The wind was beginning to moan and Septimus was glad to put on the cloak.

He came to the top of a rounded hill and the lane led out from under the trees on to an open heath where it forked. He got out the pencil torch that he always carried and examined the ground. There were fresh hoof marks on the left fork. He guessed it curved down to the border and trudged on, downhill now with the track becoming very muddy as it plunged into a wooded valley with a noisy stream at the bottom. There was no bridge over the stream.

He paused to have a drink and freshen his face with the ice-cold water. He suddenly realized that he was tired and hungry, and his injured shoulder was aching. He sat down on a boulder and got out his pipe. The rider on the black horse must be far ahead by now, but Septimus had stayed alive in the war so far by taking no unnecessary risks. He made a light-proof tent over his head with the cloak, applied match to pipe bowl, and smoked peacefully with his hand clasped over the pipe in order to mask the glow. He reviewed the events of the crowded evening, assessing what progress he had made.

According to Captain McLeod, the affair was bigger than just a leak about H_2S—though that was certainly serious enough. He looked at his watch. It was half past one. In less than twenty-four hours he had stumbled on one villain who was now dead, pursued a second into neutral territory, and was now following a third back into the UK. By the prompt action which had been taken against him at the Royal George, it was clear that there must be efficient communication with the scientific establishment at Malvern—and that meant another traitor. There were the two muscle men —Tweedledum and Tweedledee—whom he had pushed into the dock, and presumably the landlord of the Royal George as well. That added up to seven at least—and that was presuming the Red Cow at Killegaran was nothing more than a convenient meeting place. To all that had to be added efficient contact with the German Embassy in Dublin. It looked like a large and high-powered organization, and so far he had only touched the edge of it.

He tapped out his pipe, removed his shoes and socks, rolled up his trousers and waded the stream, wincing both at the coldness of the water and the stoniness of the bottom.

He dried himself sketchily on the cloak, replaced his footgear and set off up the side of the valley. The lane narrowed beyond the stream to a mere track. It was steep and wooded, the trees pressing close over the path, so that he was breathless and hot by the time he had climbed from the valley on to another bare shoulder of hill.

The wind was strong and keen now. The clouds had blown away and the moon was low over the rounded hills. Septimus paused, catching his breath, gazing up at a million stars and the majestic sweep of the Milky Way against the polished blue vault of outer space. It made him feel small and the dangers that surrounded him seemed unimportant. If not on this investigation, then on another, he would die as Fieldman had died twenty-four hours previously, as at that moment men were dying all over the world for things that the politicians said were important. And if the war didn't do for him, some criminal would, or he would walk under a bus, and the world would go on in its own crazy way as if Septimus Treloar had never lived. He grinned slowly at the night and then winked at the Pole Star. 'Septimus,' he said out loud, 'you're getting morbid.'

Twice more the track divided, but each time it was easy to follow the horse's tracks. So at last, desperately weary, he came down a long valley which widened before him as the sky began to lighten in the east. The valley flattened, and the track became a broad ride of smooth, sheep-nibbled grass. Then there was a turn by a large barn, hedges again, and finally a gate which led to a metalled road. He climbed the gate and set off to the right, limping now on blistered feet, his shoulder burning like fire, conscious of his muddy condition, hopeful but not absolutely sure that he had crossed the border in the night. Half a mile down the road he passed a sizeable farm with a horse-drawn trap in the yard and the clanking of milk churns coming from the cowshed. Just beyond the farm a lane led off to the right, and he was relieved to see a small signpost on the grass verge: 'RAF TW Unit 63.' Up in the hills against the coming day he could see the lonely finger of a radio mast. Well, at least he wasn't going to have to break out of an Irish police station.

Behind him there was the sound of a horse and iron-shod wheels—the trap from the farm was following him along the road. He waved to the driver, and as the man reined in his horse he said, 'Morning. Are you going into Londonderry?'

'Aye. That's right. Milk for the station. You wanting a lift?'

'You bet,' said Septimus, climbing aboard, and too eager to be aware of the unclerical nature of the reply.

The farmer glanced at him with curiosity. 'You look as if you've had a wild night, mister.' Septimus agreed.

'But then, you're a Catholic,' said the man, as if that explained the black-clad, mud-covered scarecrow. He ruminated as the pony jogged along, and then added, 'My missus belongs to the Free Pentecostal Church in Derry. Me, I'm an atheist, and you're a Catholic father.'

Septimus replied in the same oracular vein. 'Quite so. But then things are not always what they seem, and I'll give you ten shillings if you'll drive me to the narrow-gauge railway station before you deliver your milk.'

The bargain was struck, and Septimus fell into a half-simulated doze in order to avoid further conversation.

So he arrived back in Londonderry as the city was being shaken into wakefulness by the clatter of milkmen and the tramp of postmen's boots. His van was still waiting in the cul-de-sac and he changed thankfully out of his clerical disguise, so that as he drove past the guardroom at Maydown the top half of him looked like a perfectly respectable, if unshaven, army officer.

In his cabin he removed his shoes and fell fast asleep on top of the bedclothes.

7

Admirals and Other Ranks

Septimus, riding a black horse and wearing a torn raincoat, was being pursued along a narrow-gauge railway line by a herd of pigs. He awoke from his dream because someone was shaking his shoulder. He opened his eyes and looked up into a smiling face, a wide, pretty face with freckles and surrounded by a mass of dark curls.

'Hullo,' he said sleepily. 'What's your name?'

'Pamela, sir. Pamela Byrnes. I'm the steward that looks after you.' Her big eyes strayed to his mud-plastered trousers. 'I didn't wake you early, sir, because—well—you looked as if you'd had a busy night. But I've brought you a cup of tea.' Her mouth was wide, her grin friendly, her accent middle-class with a hardness in the vowels which Septimus placed in Manchester. He accepted the cup of tea gratefully and heaved himself off the bed, wincing at the pain in his shoulder. He surveyed his unshaven face with disfavour in the mirror. It was ugly at the best of times, and mud and black bristles did not improve it.

The tea was hot and sweet and Septimus gulped it gratefully.

'You and I are going to get on well together, Pamela,' he said.

'Yes, sir,' she replied, busy with the bed. 'I'll get you a clean pillowcase. This one's muddy.' He looked round for his shaving kit, a little surprised that such an efficient young lady had not unpacked for him. He opened Sergeant Dickinson's case which lay where he had left it on the table. Sleepily he glanced at the number counter at the back of the left-hand lock. With a jerk he came fully awake. The number was wrong. The case had been opened.

'Pamela,' he asked abruptly, 'have you opened this case?'

She heard the urgency in his voice and turned to him in some alarm. 'Certainly not, sir. Of course I usually unpack for the officers, but I thought I'd better leave it—you being a security man.'

'Quite right,' he replied absently. 'I keep a rattlesnake in it to protect my combinations.' So . . . as at Malvern, someone had been through his room. Evidently one of the Maydown part of the spy ring. A Wren steward or an officer would be least conspicuous in the cabin block. He must warn Sam as soon as possible not only about the possibility of another agent at Malvern, but also about what looked like the existence of a much more sophisticated and swifter means of communication across the Irish Sea than the mere exchange of letters.

'Is there anything wrong, sir?' Pamela interrupted his train of thought.

'No,' he replied, turning to her, suddenly coming to a decision. The basic principle of counter-espionage work was to trust no one; but he had come to a decision to break the rules, to trust this girl with the wide mouth and the pleasant smile. He could not for the life of him have said why.

'Pamela, I need your help.' She waited, saying nothing while he arranged his ideas.

'You know that my job is security.' She nodded. 'Well, it's not just looking at barbed wire and stopping the RAF getting into the Wrennery. It's a great deal more serious. I can't tell you what, but it's to do with Rory McLusky's experimental flight—and it matters.'

She waited, her freckled face full of curiosity.

'You want to help?'

'Yes.'

'Well, first off, go across to the sick bay and use your charm to get some lint, some sticking plaster and some sort of antiseptic. My shoulder wants dressing. And here's two bob. If you can find the tea wagon buy us both a cup of tea and the biggest sandwich they've got. I haven't eaten since lunchtime yesterday.'

After the girl had gone he extracted his shaving gear from the case and went along to the bathroom.

When he returned Pamela was waiting for him, the bed tidied and his muddy clothing in two neat piles, one clerical and one military. She accepted the unstewardly task of dressing his shoulder without comment and strapped up the wound efficiently. He made her sit down and drink NAAFI tea while he pottered around the cabin, climbing into the battle-dress which was the only spare uniform he possessed. He sat down, put his feet on top of the coke stove and set about the stale potted meat bread roll which was all the NAAFI wagon could produce.

He was puzzled to know how to begin. Everything he could think of sounded like an excerpt from a cheap Hollywood film. She helped him. 'That wound on your shoulder,' she said, 'it was a bullet wound.'

'Yes,' he replied, grateful that she was making it easy, 'a character pooped off a gun at me. He missed—or nearly.'

'I'm glad he missed,' she said, 'otherwise you would be dead, and that would be a pity.'

A biblical phrase floated into his mind. What was it? 'A

virtuous woman is above rubies.' He grinned at her and she couldn't help thinking he looked like a little boy.

'You're the girl I need,' he said.

She grinned back. 'I do the best I can for all my officers.'

He leaned forward and tapped her on one silk-clad knee.

'Look, Pamela,' he said, 'the job I'm on matters. Sometime last night someone came into this cabin and went through my things. Now . . . If I do my job properly and get close to an answer that someone might come to the cabin again . . .' He paused, not knowing how to phrase what he wanted to say without sounding melodramatic.

'You mean,' she said slowly, 'they might put a real rattle-snake in your case?'

'Yes,' he said, relieved that she was so quick on the uptake, 'and you see, you might find it.'

She was startled. 'Oh! I don't think I like the sound of that. What do I do, sir?'

'Well, I'll show you the basic things—like how to open the door and so on. But in general you must touch as little as possible in the room when I'm not here.'

She suddenly coloured. 'That's all very nice and fine, but what about catching the bastard?'

He could have hugged her.

'Softly, softly, catchee monkey,' he said. 'Two things. Observation: the slightest thing out of place—a hairbrush not where you put it—anything. And the other thing: I want a watch on the cabin. As near twenty-four hours as possible. You and any other Wrens you are sure you can trust. And I don't want any chatting about it in the Wrennery.'

She looked at him with cold eyes. 'No, sir,' she said.

He smiled ruefully. 'Sorry, Pamela,' he said, 'I'm afraid my business doesn't improve my manners.'

She relented and laughed. 'Wrens do chatter—just as men shoot lines. But I'll choose the ones that don't chatter because I don't think you're shooting a line.'

71

He looked at her in astonishment. While he had been sizing her up, she had been doing the same for him.

'By God, girl,' he said, 'I've a damned good mind to spank your behind.'

She laughed. 'I'll report you to the Queen Wren if you do. But if you had to cope with what I have to cope with . . . Well . . . every Swordfish that torpedoed the *Bismarck* must have had three pilots and fourteen observers.'

The sub-lieutenant paymaster in the general office which guarded the Captain's privacy was supercilious to the point of parody. He was used to fending people off, and who was this army officer in the hairy battledress?

'Yes, sir, of course. We have a priority line to Malvern, but you cannot use it without the Captain's permission.'

Septimus screwed down his irritation like the safety valve of a leaky old boiler. 'I've tried the civilian lines and I can't get through. Would you please ask the Captain.'

The supercilious sub-lieutenant sniffed. 'If you want to see the Captain, you will have to make an appointment like any-one else . . . sir.' He transferred his attention to the sheet of figures on his desk. Septimus looked down at him.

'Dear God,' he thought, 'you were in the sixth form twelve months ago.'

'I see,' he said, 'well, that's one of the things we shall have to get changed, isn't it?' He opened the door and marched into the Captain's office, hotly pursued by the young sub-lieutenant.

'Hey! You can't do that.'

Septimus grinned at him. 'I'm sorry, I just did.'

The Captain was behind his desk, Rory McLusky leaning back in an armchair.

'Ah!' said Rory. 'The perilous pongo. We were just talking about you.'

The Captain was a little irritated. 'What the devil are you doing, Treloar? You don't just walk in on me.'

'I know, sir. That's what the juvenile lead said. But it is important.'

The Captain nodded to his secretary, and the door closed behind Septimus.

'And now, Treloar, what is it?'

'I need your phone, sir. I've got to contact Malvern and my boss in London and I shall have to use a scrambler.'

'Well, since you're here, you'd better use it now, and I'll tell my secretary that you can use the priority line to Malvern.'

He pointed to the red phone on his desk. 'Help yourself.'

Septimus glanced at Rory McLusky. The Commander took the hint and heaved himself to his feet with a grin. 'By God, sir,' he said to the Captain, 'he's got me lined up as the naval Mata Hari. They're all mad, these pongos.' He walked out of the office.

McLeod looked startled. 'Good God! You don't suspect Rory McLusky?'

Septimus looked at him coolly. 'I suspect everyone, sir. That's my business.'

'Even me?'

Septimus grinned. 'Oh, your security clearance was first class, sir.' This produced an irascible snort.

'Glad to know I'm to be trusted even if one of my senior commanders isn't.'

Septimus picked up the phone. Conscious of the Captain's presence, he was more restrained than usual in his greeting to Miss Parsons. She passed him on to Sir John Masterton, and as Sir John came on the line the Captain walked out into the other office, closing the door behind him.

'That was nice of the old boy,' Septimus said, and then hastily, 'No, not you, Sir John . . .' Sir John listened in silence to Septimus's brief account of the last forty-eight hours.

'A much bigger operation than we suspected,' he said at length.

'Yes, sir.'

'I'll pass the information to Dublin. And you needn't worry about the dead clerk at Malvern. I've put a clamp on that. Do you need help?'

'Not yet, sir,' Septimus replied. 'I've got Sam Burroughs at Malvern—he's an old police colleague and he knows what he's doing. If I want help here, I'll let you know.'

As Septimus hung up the Captain came back into the office.

'I've told my secretary you're to have access to the scrambler and the Malvern priority line. Use the phone in Piggins's office—that is, if you don't think he's a spy. Oh, and Treloar, you're to see the Dockyard Admiral at fifteen hundred this afternoon.'

Piggins was not in his office, so on the strength of the Captain's instruction he helped himself to the phone. His conversation with Sam was circumspect and brief, both of them being aware of the public nature of the line. Piggins came into the office as Septimus was sitting at the Security Officer's desk, considering his next move. They went across to the wardroom for a beer.

They stood by the window watching a series of Swordfish coming in to land. They would touch down, open their throttles immediately and take off again, roaring low over the wardroom.

'Dummy deck landings,' said Piggins. 'That's the anti-submarine squadron working up for carrier operations.'

Septimus watched the procession of aircraft and the antics of the batsman with his two paddles on the edge of the runway.

'They don't carry the really secret stuff, do they?' he said.

Piggins looked at Septimus, his eyes sharp.

'No. That's entirely Rory McLusky's business. The A/S boys have nothing to do with it.'

'And how do you look after the stuff?' Septimus asked. 'I mean an ordinary security fence isn't much protection against marauders.'

74

Piggins pointed. 'That's the radio workshop over there, opposite the guardroom. It's only got one door which faces the guardroom entrance.'

Septimus nodded. 'Well placed. What about the windows?'

'They're barred on the inside—and the blackout shutters are on the outside, and they're left open unless the radio mechanics are working late. The police have special instructions to keep an eye on the place.'

'That seems fair enough,' said Septimus. 'What happens when the wizard's boxes are in the aircraft?'

'We don't leave them in the aircraft overnight. They're easy enough to remove, and I got a directive from the Captain that they always have to be returned to the workshop after flights. Had a hell of an argument with Jerry Haines, the Radio Officer. Said it was bad for 'em, taking 'em in and out like yo-yos. But McLusky supported me.'

'Sounds like a good set-up,' said Septimus. 'Simple and effective. I like it.' But the trouble with simple arrangements was that they might have a simple and very large hole in them. He could not imagine what it could be, but he viewed the radio workshop with some reserve.

On his way to Londonderry to keep his appointment with the Admiral Septimus stopped his van outside the radio workshop. He walked round the outside, noting the heavy shutters; then stood in the road, considering the unpretentious building of curved corrugated iron raised from the ground on brick piles. It was like so many thousand similar temporary buildings; ugly but functional. He went up the steps and opened the door, taking note of the lock as he did so.

Inside there were four radio mechanics working at benches and a pale young man with spectacles who looked exactly what he was—a highly skilled radio engineer temporarily dressed up as a naval officer. Septimus explained himself and the young man smiled nervously. He was disposed to be helpful.

'I'm Jerry Haines,' he said. 'Piggy Piggins said I might expect a call from you. All about the Hun trying to pinch the wizard's boxes—H2S and O4, that is.'

'That and other things,' Septimus replied easily. 'But I am interested in your wizard's boxes. After all, Hitler's not likely to be interested in the specifications of a Swordfish. How would you set about pinching one of your own secrets?'

Haines was serious. 'I've given it a good deal of thought. If anyone actually pinched one I'd notice. The wiring diagrams wouldn't be much use because they only show the connections and not the really secret bits. You'd have to take photographs —but I don't see how that could be done in the day with my people around. And I don't see how you could do it at night. Honestly, I think about the only person who could do it is me—and I don't intend to.'

Haines showed Septimus some of the secret equipment— boxes, grey rather than black, covered with dials and knobs which were meaningless to Septimus. He wandered round the workshop, noting the security of the windows, a possibility forming in his mind.

'What about keys to the door?' he asked.

'There are two,' Haines replied. 'I keep one, and there's one on the master board in the guardroom.' Septimus was standing by a bench apparently watching a radio mechanic doing a particularly delicate piece of soldering, while in fact he was examining the bench at which the man was working. He moved down the bench, apparently to get a better view. Then he thanked Haines and left the workshop.

That bench was a good eight feet long, built against the wall, and with solid ends where it abutted on storage cupboards. There had been pinholes in the edge of the bench top. Just pinholes in the wood, but he could only imagine one reason for their presence. Suppose an agent wanted to photograph secret equipment? He could not do it by day, and by night he would be unable to black out the workshop because the shutters were on the outside and the guardroom opposite.

But it would be possible to make a light-proof box under the bench.

It seemed improbable, but however he tried he could think of no other reason for that neat series of pinholes. In the confined space under the bench would it be possible to get the camera far enough away from what you were photographing? Could it be done at all? He was not sure. The only thing to do was to try. And if he got caught? His lips twitched into a little smile. They all thought he was a security-mad 'pongo' anyway.

The entrance to the Royal Dockyard was two minutes' walk from the Royal George. Septimus showed his pass at the gate and was given directions for the Admiral's office. Carefully he negotiated the seemingly chaotic activity of the place: cranes, trucks, piles of drums, heaps of rusty chain, with civilians and naval personnel hurrying along the unguarded edges of the quays. He passed a minesweeper with a smoke-blackened hole in its fo'c'sle and a gang of men working with oxy-acetylene torches, cutting away wreckage, flinging it clanging on to the jetty. He glanced sideways at the crane which was hovering like some prehistoric monster over the minesweeper, his eye travelling down the boom to the driver in his cab. It was Tweedledee—the tall thin one of the two men he had pushed into the dock outside the Royal George. Hastily he drove on, turning away his head, not wanting to be recognized, the pattern beginning to take shape in his mind: Malvern, Maydown and the Naval Dockyard; no doubt the escort vessels which surrounded him used the secret products of the scientists' brains.

The Rear Admiral was a large man with a shock of white hair and a manner which was a mixture of one who had spent much time in command of ships of war, and the easy courtesy of a man accustomed to the duties and privileges of high command. As Captain McLeod had prophesied, he talked a good deal about sabotage in the dockyard. Septimus was not greatly interested in this. After all, if you had to use a naval base in such a disaffected part of the Empire as Ulster, it was hardly surprising that there were plenty of people to put extraneous bolts into turbines because they disliked the English even more than the Germans.

He couched his thought in polite terms. 'Yes, sir. But my main brief is H2S and O4. What about them?' The Admiral was a little taken aback by the abruptness of the question.

'I'm not supposed to talk about them . . . But seeing you are who you are . . . Yes, well. We've tried H2S out over a convoy in the Western Approaches. Very promising. But the airmen weren't too happy about the definition. So it went back to Malvern and they adapted it to our special needs.'

'O4,' said Septimus.

'Yes. That's right. I gather from McLeod it's ready and we are planning to try it out over another convoy.'

'Only one, sir?' Septimus asked.

'Only one. But if it's all that my staff say it is, it could make all the difference to the Battle of the Atlantic.' Septimus thought about this for a moment. He had experience of that grim battle of fire and freezing water, of high explosives and men groping for one another in the dark. He had been sent to America six months previously. It was not an experiment he wanted to repeat.

The Admiral looked at his watch. 'Anything more I can do for you, Treloar?'

'Two things, sir. I've got a lead on the people working in the dockyard. So I'd like to be able to come down here and not look conspicuous. Can your people lend me the sort of heavy duty top clothing issued to civilian workers? And can I have a word with someone who could supply me with the name and address of one of your crane drivers?'

The Admiral picked up the phone and such is the power of high command that both requests were arranged in two minutes, and Septimus was met outside the Admiral's office by a taciturn Ulsterman wearing a shiny blue suit and a bowler hat.

They went first to the police office where Septimus was issued with a pass in his own name, but with his job concealed. Then they went to a clothing store where he found himself a grimy donkey jacket of heavy blue serge, a pair of steel-toed industrial boots, and a battered protective helmet.

Lastly the two of them concealed themselves behind a pile of crates and the taciturn gentleman told Septimus that the crane driver's name was Seamus McColin. He consulted a list and gave his address as 25 Larne Street. Septimus thanked him and returned to his van.

When he got back to the officers' block at Maydown, Pamela Byrnes came out of the stewards' pantry at the end of the corridor.

'Oh, sir,' she said. 'I sent your uniform to be cleaned. But I didn't know what to do with the other stuff—the clerical rig.'

He asked her to get them cleaned and returned to the cathedral. He scribbled a note of apology and gave her three pounds to include in the parcel. 'Oh, and Pamela,' he said, 'you can return the clerical collar to the padre.'

'Yes, sir,' she said with a friendly grin curling her wide mouth. 'You do seem to have been having a holy time.' She obviously thought the whole affair very funny. For Septimus's part he found her very pretty, and was glad to see the smile on her face beneath the dark hair.

'Who's responsible for blackout curtains here on the camp?' he asked.

'First Officer Buchanan, sir. But the curtain you cut up isn't one of hers, is it? She'd be very cross.'

'No, it isn't. It belonged to the Catholic Church—so you must treat it with reverence—even if it has got a hole in it.'

Instructed by Pamela he found First Officer Buchanan in a little office attached to the Clothing Store. Yes, she was responsible for blackout curtains, and yes, she did have a lot of them because there were a lot of windows in the camp; but she failed to see why she should lend yards of it to any stray army officer who turned up at the door. It took all of Septimus's formidable charm, together with the sight of one of his more impressive identity cards and the iron hand of a threat to ring the Captain in the velvet glove of a joke, before he managed to get what he wanted from a very determined young lady.

Next, he went to the wardroom and while he drank a cup of tea stole the box of drawing pins from the shelf beneath the wardroom notice board. Back in his cabin he persuaded Pamela to borrow a holdall large enough to take the black cloth he had extracted from First Officer Buchanan.

'You've got a fixation about blackout cloth,' she said.

'Yes,' he replied. 'My mother was frightened by a black parson in an air-raid shelter when she was expecting me.' She went off laughing while he went to bed.

His alarm clock woke him at seven-thirty when he knew most of the officers would be in the wardroom and the other ranks at supper. He packed the blackout material into the canvas holdall and took it, with his document case, out to the van. He drove down to the main gate and parked outside the radio workshop. He made an ostentatious show of trying to open the door, conscious that the policeman by the gate was watching him; then he walked across to the guardroom where the guard were sitting round the table eating their supper.

'The key to the radio workshop,' he said to the duty Petty Officer, 'I was in there this afternoon talking to the Radio Officer and I must have put my document case down.' Septimus knew exactly what would happen. Army, RAF or Navy, the procedure was always the same. It was the business of the duty NCO to issue the keys to anyone who had a right to them, to see that they were signed for in the ledger and their return acknowledged in the same ledger—and there his duty ended. Nothing was further from his mind than security.

He was probably thinking about something altogether different.

The Petty Officer went to the glass-fronted keyboard and handed Septimus a key attached to a large brass tag, indicating where he should sign in the ledger. He returned to his supper without so much as glancing at the key, which was superficially no different from the hundred others on the board. Septimus thanked him and walked across the road and round the back of his van, picking up his document case and holdall. He carried them close and low so that they were concealed by his body and the van from both the guardroom and the policeman on the gate. He unlocked the door and went into the workshop. He hid the holdall behind a piece of testing equipment, then removed the key from its ring, substituting the useless Yale which had once opened the front door of his now non-existent flat. He walked back out, carrying the document case under his arm, carefully locking and testing the door. He returned the key tag with the wrong key to the guardroom, signed that he had returned it, and drove to the wardroom for dinner.

8

High Security

The alarm clock which he had put under his pillow to deaden the sound awoke him at two o'clock. It was dark outside, the moon obscured by the heavy overcast, a light rain falling. He dressed quickly, putting on his black roll-neck sweater, balaclava helmet, trousers and gym shoes, slipping the tools he would need into a canvas bag which looped on to his belt. He went silently out of his cabin, along the corridor and out into the darkness and the rain.

There were no lights visible. He moved softly along the grass outside the huts, keeping to the shadows, until he came to the perimeter track round the airfield. He crossed it and made a wide detour out on to the wet grass away from the buildings, and then turned back to the rear of the radio workshop. He crawled underneath the building, inching forward in the dry and dusty darkness, taking care not to dislodge any of the loose rubble, moving so silently that he could hear the drip of the rain from the corrugated iron and the soft swish it made on the grass as the wind blew it.

He reached the front of the building and lay behind the steps, looking out. The door of the guardroom was open, a dim oblong of blue from the night lighting. There was the sound of slow pacing on the tarmac and a man strolled past moving in the direction of the gate. As he passed the blue oblong of the door, Septimus saw from his silhouette that he was a policeman. The footsteps moved on towards the gate and then stopped. There was a murmur of voices and the flare of a match held in cupped hands briefly illuminating two faces, white in the sudden glare, one of them framed in the haloed circle of a steel helmet. The match went out, then there was the occasional brief glow of the cigarettes.

Septimus crawled from under the hut, flitted up the steps, and was in the workshop in less than three seconds and with hardly a sound. He took his pencil torch from the bag and shielding its bright beam to the merest glimmer between his fingers, he crawled across the floor to retrieve the canvas holdall from its hiding place. Working as quickly and silently as was possible in the darkness, he unrolled the blackout material and pinned a treble thickness to the top and legs of the bench, laying an extra thickness along the edge of the bench top and down the ends, leaving himself an opening like a tent flap. He picked up one of the H2S sets and carried it to his tent opening. It was difficult to manoeuvre the heavy set through the opening and get himself in after it, but he managed with only a few faint scraping noises and one bump of his head. He pinned the blackout cloth securely from the inside, then paused a moment, regaining his breath and looking at his watch. It was just before half past two. He had plenty of time before the guard changed.

He positioned the H2S at one end of his stuffy hiding place, its screen and dials toward him, and put his watch on top of it. The watch with its illuminated dial would give him an aiming point for the camera. He took the camera from his canvas bag—a camera which at a casual glance looked like a cigarette case—and a flash attachment no bigger than an egg cup. He took great care about the lens settings, then switched off the torch and waited for his night vision to return—until he could see the illuminated dial of his watch. It was difficult to line up the camera, but he managed it. As he pressed the knob he closed his eyes against the glare of the flash bulb. He took two more exposures of the front of the set, then turned it round and took two of the back. With a screwdriver from his pack he removed the back cover of the set and took two shots of the interior, sweating now with the heat and stuffiness of his hiding place.

As he guessed they would be, the working parts of the set were designed to slide partly out of the case for ease of maintenance. He eased them out, took six more exposures—two from each of three angles—then he replaced the back and with the help of his torch made a note of all the serial and mark numbers he could find on the case. Only then did he allow himself to wipe his streaming brow on the back of his sleeve and look again at his watch. It was ten past three.

He slid gratefully from under the bench into the comparatively fresh air of the workshop, replaced all as he had found it and crept cautiously to the door, Pamela's canvas bag in his hand.

He stood silent, absolutely motionless, a blacker shadow in

the darkness of the workshop for a full three minutes. He opened the door the merest crack. All was as it had been before: the softly falling rain, the blue rectangle of the guardroom door. There was the merest suggestion of light to the east, and a man coughed somewhere on the road. In the guardroom someone was snoring loudly. Septimus smiled. It was such a homely sound. He slipped out on to the steps, the rain soft and cold on his face, closing the door behind him. In one smooth movement he went down the steps, round the corner and along the side of the hut, running lightly now, and so away across the darkness of the airfield.

Ten minutes later he climbed thankfully into bed, and as he did so a cock on a nearby farm heralded a premature dawn.

Septimus got up early, a little puzzled not to have heard the sounds of reveille at six-thirty—until, with a grimace at his own forgetfulness, he remembered that it was Sunday when the Navy allowed itself an extra hour in what he supposed the men called their hammocks. When Pamela Byrnes knocked at the door and came in with a cup of tea and his cleaned and pressed uniform, she found him standing naked to the waist trying, very awkwardly, to put a plaster on his shoulder.

'Good morning, sir.' Without comment she went up to him and took the plaster from him. It was a warm, feminine gesture with no hint of silliness which endeared her to Septimus. She saw the damp and dirty clothing of his night's foray in a heap on the floor. 'I see you've been out on the tiles again, sir. I'll get that lot cleaned up.' He thanked her, asked her to return the blackout material to First Officer Buchanan and walked out into a fitfully bright morning with the early sun challenging the thinning clouds in the sky of blue and white marble. He marched off in the direction of the main gate, upright in his clean uniform, purposeful, and very military.

There was a different Chief Petty Officer on duty this morning. He was a stocky sort of man with a square face and a soft Devonshire accent. Septimus played to perfection the alert young officer, keen on clobbering the Hun.

'Ah! Chief! Good morning! Lovely morning. What's the naval phrase?—"The sun's burning your eyes out"?'

The Chief viewed this military apparition with disfavour. He had been up half the night, had not had a chance to shave, had not breakfasted, and in a long service career had seen far too many keen and alert young officers.

'Yes, sir. They do say that. So I'm told. And what can I do for you, sir?'

'You've heard of me? Name of Treloar. Here on a special job. Routine security check.'

A lurid phrase which had been used at the bar in the PO's mess the previous evening floated into the Chief's mind, but he kept it to himself, contenting himself with a polite, 'Yes, sir, I had heard.' He waited patiently while Septimus explained in keen military phrases how he had been running a security check on the radio workshop.

'I got into the workshop last night and set up certain— well—checks and tests. Can't tell you what. Jolly old security you know, Chief, that was what I was up to. Well—if Adolf knew what we were up to—there wouldn't be any point in being up to it.' The point of all this drivel was that Septimus wanted the key to the radio workshop and the presence of the Chief.

The Chief agreed readily enough. He wanted his breakfast, and long experience had taught him that the best way with the Septimus's of this world was to agree with everything that they said. That way you got over it in the shortest possible time.

Solemnly Septimus signed for the key and the two of them crossed the road. While the Chief examined the shutters down one side of the hut Septimus went down the other—using the opportunity to replace the correct key on the ring. They met at the door, examined the lock with due solemnity, entered, and subjected the barred windows to a totally pointless

85

inspection—although it did give Septimus the chance to re-trieve a stray drawing pin: the only sign he could discover of his night's activities.

So at last, the solemn farce concluded, the key was duly returned to the board, Septimus signed it back in, and the Chief watched him march off down the road.

'Silly bugger,' he said.

Well satisfied with himself, Septimus went to the eight o'clock Communion Service in the Nissen hut which served as a chapel.

After breakfast Septimus met up with Rory McLusky and an observer whom he did not know outside the wardroom. Both men were partially clad in flying kit, and Rory introduced the observer as Pat Samuels.

'I didn't think the Navy fought the war on Sundays,' said Septimus.

'We don't,' Pat replied. 'We're off to Malvern for a dirty weekend.'

'Just the place,' Septimus replied, thinking of the Spa hotels and the largely retired population. Then more tenta-tively, fishing for information, 'Another of the wizard's boxes?'

Rory McLusky was noncommittal. 'Could be. I spend most of my life running a taxi service between here and Malvern.'

Septimus walked with them to the hardstanding outside the hangar where the Swordfish Gertie was already running up, making the closed hangar doors rattle with the roar of her engine. Were they, he wondered, going to collect O4? If so, he would have to revise his plans.

'When will you be back?' he asked.

'Probably stay overnight and whoop it up in the Abbey Hotel,' said Pat Samuels.

Rory McLusky snorted. 'Abbey crypt more like. What are you going to do, Septimus?'

'Thought I might justify my existence by walking round your perimeter wire. Count the number of holes—and after all, it's a nice day.'

'Take my dog with you,' said McLusky. 'That Wren popsy in the cabin block—Pamela Byrnes—she looks after him while I'm away. Make good company—both of them.'

Septimus stood on the edge of the tarmac and watched Gertie trundle away to the end of the runway, holding his cap as the slipstream caught him. The aircraft paused, accelerated, and then in a remarkably short distance was airborne and the noise of its engine dwindled into the distance.

Septimus found Flight-Lieutenant Piggins reading the Sunday paper in front of the wardroom fire. His new-found urgency made him abrupt so that he greatly startled the poor man.

'You'll have to leave that Sunday scandal rag, Piggins. You've got some securing to do.' The air force officer got up, wondering what horrible gap in his defences this army officer had discovered. Septimus led him from the wardroom, explaining as they went what was needed. It was not an easy assignment. There were no photographers available as it was a Sunday, so eventually they had to help themselves to the facilities of the laboratory and dark-room.

Septimus would not explain as he set about developing and printing his film. It was a business he had had to learn, but he was no expert and did not wish to commit himself fully until he saw the result of his spying activities. He passed the time questioning the other man about the other officers who might have a conceivable excuse to enter the radio workshop. It seemed that half the officers in the camp—and a fair number of other ranks: wireless operators, observers, telegraphist rear-gunners, old Uncle Tom Cobleigh and all—used the workshop for making or mending their own radios. They probably used service equipment as well, but that was the concern of Piggins and Haines and no business of his. O4 was his worry, and his concern showed in his language so that he alarmed Piggins even more.

At last the developing was done, and in silence Septimus laid the wet prints in front of the Security Officer. Considering the difficult circumstances under which they had been taken, they were really quite creditable.

'Oh, my God,' said Piggins in abject horror, 'where did you get these?'

For good measure, and to drive the lesson home, Septimus added the notes he had taken of the serial and mark numbers.

'You know what it is?' he asked grimly.

'Yes. It's H2S.' Piggins put his head in his hands. 'They'll court martial me. Chuck me out of the service.'

Septimus relented. 'No, they won't. Because I took them last night. Just to show how easy it was. How it could have been done.'

The other man stared at him. 'You? But how?'

Septimus explained, and then concluded, 'And what I can do, anybody else could do. And quite apart from all the names in the keybook—yours included, my lad—there are pinholes in the frame of that bench.'

Piggins looked at him miserably. 'What shall I do?' he asked.

'First you can make a list of people really allowed in that workshop and see that no one else—but no one else—goes in. Then you can put a twenty-four-hour guard on the door. You can tell the Captain I suggested it because there's more secret equipment due from Malvern.' He smiled, relenting at the sight of the other man's wretchedness. 'That'll keep you busy for the rest of the day, so I'll burn these prints—and the negatives and notes, and then we can both forget about it.'

Rory McLusky's dog proved to be a nondescript black creature of vaguely spaniel origin and of zany habits. It suffered under the name of 'Piddle'.

'If that dog were mine,' said Pamela as she and Septimus

walked up the lane together, 'I should change its name.' Septimus smiled. An army officer and a Wren running across the Irish landscape and shouting 'Piddle!' had infinite possibilities.

He had picked up Pamela and the dog half a mile from the camp (Wrens walking out with officers from their own camps was not considered by the Navy to be ladylike behaviour); and they had left Septimus's van in the lane leading to the RAF TW unit. Septimus justified this misuse of service petrol on the perfectly reasonable ground that he wanted to explore the border track—which he had walked along in the middle of the night—by daylight.

It was a beautiful warm spring day, with a few fleecy clouds white as the lambs in the fields on the rounded hills which rose blue as smoke to their left. It was a day to think about new life; about love and about laughter rather than about espionage and the drab, dangerous boredom of war. Septimus wondered with a sort of innocent amazement as they strolled along why on earth men put up with it. Why did he put up with it? Getting shot at, and having various clever characters working out ingenious ways to kill him? *Dulce et decorum est pro patria mori*. But was it? If you asked any of the embattled Germans, Italians, Britons, Americans, Russians and Japanese over the face of the globe what they would really like to do on this particular May morning, he was convinced they would almost all have said, 'I want to go home.' Was it the politicians? Was it Original Sin? Or was it just plain human stupidity and cussedness? He hadn't the slightest idea. In the meantime he would enjoy Pamela's charming company and keep a weather eye on his job.

He was by nature a man who lived fully in the present moment, and it was very pleasant to stroll in this enchanted countryside with a very pretty young woman. He wanted to learn about her, and encouraged her to talk about herself and her home, slashing at the thistles in the hedgerows with a borrowed walking stick as they strolled along.

She was the daughter of a country doctor who had a practice in the high Pennines above Manchester. She was knowledgeable about birds and animals and told him much he did not know about the ways of badgers. She owned a horse called Mangas Colorado, a Welsh cob, which she had been much grieved to leave behind when she joined the Wrens. She had done a year at Manchester University studying 'Home Economics'.

'Why "Home Economics"? ' he asked. 'Do you have to go to university to make a successful wife and mother?'

She laughed at him. 'You're a stuffy old thing, Septimus. Too much playing at cops and robbers! You sound like a bearded Victorian father of thirteen, talking about the little woman's place being in the home.'

He was instantly repentant. 'Sorry,' he said. 'That was pompous. Too much male society. But why "Home Economics" then?'

'When the war's over I'm going to run a highly expensive hotel, and when I've made a fortune I shall buy a yacht and explore the world.' She paused, suddenly serious, her mouth drooping. ' "We are as near to God by sea as by land." '

'What's that?' he asked, aware that it meant much to her and conscious of his own ignorance.

'Sir Humphrey Gilbert,' she said, 'in a ten-ton pinnace off the Azores. That was what he said in the face of a storm. I'd like to see the world I live in before I die. But what about you?'

He found it difficult to express things that he felt but had hardly ever articulated, but she encouraged him. He talked of his brigadier father, who now worked in the War Office, and of his six brothers—most of them scattered through the world in the forces, and of his Cornish home—now commandeered by the Army. He told her about his mother, whom he remembered only as a dim and loving presence from his infancy. Then of the years in the police: the slow rise from the rank of constable; what it was like to pound the beat in the East End of London.

'So that's why you're called Septimus,' she said. 'You were the seventh. I wondered why.'

He laughed. 'After my brother Adam—he's with the Eighth Army—my father just numbered us off from the left.'

'But didn't your mother mind?'

'Oh, yes. But it didn't make much difference.'

They passed the farm where Septimus had heard the milk churns in the early dawn and came to the gate that led to the track over the border. He opened the gate.

'Where are we going?' she asked.

'I thought it looked nice here,' he replied innocently.

'Liar,' she said.

They turned the corner by the big barn and came to the wide, straight section which led to the bottom of the valley.

'I know what this is,' Pamela said, 'it's the bottom end of an old drovers' road. I bet it leads over the hills into the Free State.'

'Yes, it does,' said Septimus. 'But how do you know it's a drovers' road?'

'You get the same sort of thing in the Pennines,' she replied. 'Tracks over the hills for cattle. They used to bring them over the border from Scotland. And often at the bottom end you get a nice grassy bit. I suppose they used to rest the cattle before taking them to market. We're not very far from Derry. I bet they brought them over the border and shipped them to England.'

'Makes sense,' he said, withdrawing into himself. It made sense as a wartime channel of communication across a neutral border. In this land of horses and donkeys, what more innocent than a man riding in the hills?

He was brought back to the present by a sudden shout of 'Piddle!' from Pamela.

To the left, the flat 'ride' was broken with molehills and rocky outcrops: the vegetation was rough—bracken, gorse and brambles. The ludicrously named 'Piddle' was in headlong career after a rabbit. He was barking hysterically, and

91

clumsily trying to follow the zigzag evasion of the cotton-wool tail in front of his nose.

'Come on,' said Pamela urgently, 'we mustn't lose him.' They set off in pursuit. Rabbit and dog came out on a winding path which led toward the hedge beyond the broken ground. Suddenly the rabbit dived into a bramble bush and disappeared from sight. Presumably it had gone to earth. 'Piddle' cast around and then set off excitedly, nose close down on a false trail, along the path. They followed, cursing, laughing, shouting the ridiculous name. The path ended at a gate in the hedge. The dog stopped a moment, looked back at them, and then slipped over the bottom bar of the gate and disappeared.

'Must lead to a farm,' said Pamela. 'Come on. If that confounded animal gets among the farmer's lambs he'll get himself shot.'

A hundred yards beyond the gate they came to the yard of a small farm: the usual whitewashed doll's house of a building, with four rooms symmetrically round a door, and a range of tumble-down outbuildings round a muddy yard. A man in leather gaiters was standing on the back doorstep—clearly the farmer. Crooked over his arm he was holding a shotgun broken at the breach, and he was stooping, fondling the ears of the affectionate and idiotic 'Piddle'. He stood up as they approached and what might have started as a smile of welcome changed midway into a scowl.

'This your dog?' he asked, his tone unfriendly. Pamela drew breath to explain and apologize, but she was forestalled by Septimus.

'Yes,' he said with his most innocent smile. 'At least he belongs to a friend of mine. But you see, he's out flying today, so we agreed to exercise him.'

'You should keep him on a lead,' growled the farmer.

'We're sorry about that,' said Septimus, sounding genuinely penitent, 'but he chased after a rabbit and got ahead of us. We were wondering if you would be so kind as to sell us a glass of milk. Just the thing for a lovely spring day—a glass of milk fresh from the farm.' Looking at him, Pamela had an urge to giggle. He made her think of a big brown bear contemplating an accessible beehive.

'No, I can't,' said the farmer. Then, relenting a little, 'I don't keep cows, only sheep.'

It was a patent untruth, but Septimus merely replied, 'Oh, what a pity. Still, never mind. But I wonder if you'd mind if we continued our walk down your front drive? I expect it comes out in the lane leading to the RAF site. Make a round trip for us.'

'No, you can't,' said the farmer sourly, 'on account of the sheep and that dog.'

'We'd keep the dog on a lead—promise.'

'Look, mister, I said "no". So take your dog and get off my land by the way you came.'

Pamela was furious. 'You ill-mannered lout,' she said over her shoulder as she collected the subdued Piddle who, with the mysterious instinct of his kind, had sensed trouble. She and Septimus retraced their steps. For Pamela the uncouth incident was a dark cloud on an otherwise golden afternoon; for Septimus it was a cause for furious thought.

When they got back to the van, instead of turning down the lane for Maydown, Septimus turned right up the rutted lane. 'Let's go and see if the RAF will give us a cup of tea,' he said. They passed the front entrance to the inhospitable farm: a reasonably tidy five-bar gate with the name painted on it—'Perrins'.

The corporal and the two radio operators who were the duty crew in the wooden hut at the base of the tall masts were glad to see them and glad of an excuse to brew tea. Theirs was a boring and lonely job, especially on Sundays; so the kettle was boiled on top of the inevitable coke stove and the tea served in the inevitable chipped enamel mugs.

While the tea was brewing Septimus borrowed a pair of RAF binoculars and went outside to survey the countryside.

The RAF site had been chosen for its command of the surrounding area, and from this high vantage point Septimus could see much of the drovers' road as it led up from the road gate, past the barn, along the flat portion, up into the hills, and then disappeared, presumably over the border into Eire. But his real interest was the farm they had just visited, a small white oblong among the soft green of the fields, its front drive leading straight from the lane, the track at the rear joining up with the drovers' road. Close to the farmhouse there was a paddock with three horses and two donkeys in it. One of the horses was black. Septimus watched it intently for two minutes as it stood ruminating under a tree, gently swishing its tail. At last it moved, turning its rump toward him. He dropped the binoculars on their lanyard and stood very still for several seconds. There was a patch of white on one of its back legs.

9

Perrins

The blackout at Perrins was not good: the curtains were not thick enough, nor did they meet in the middle. But that, Septimus reflected as he crept along in the shadow of the hedge, was only what you would expect this far from air-raid wardens and so close to the border.

It was ten-thirty. Clouds were blowing up from the west, threatening the usual Irish rain after the brief spring day. After parting from Pamela, Septimus had dined in the wardroom, mildly amused to have his leg pulled by a joking crowd of junior officers who found the idea of an armed sentry on the radio workshop hilariously funny. Pleasant young men, he thought, interested only in flying: young men for whom everything to do with the war had to be treated as a joke. It was, he recognized, an attitude which had its point. There were more ways of courting sudden death than counter-espionage—and flying totally outdated aeroplanes was certainly one of them.

An owl swooped low over his head, hooted in reproach at his unexpected presence, and swept away over the hedgerow on silent wings. He paused by a convenient gap and surveyed the front of the farm through binoculars. They disclosed no light other than that in the one window which he took to be the kitchen. He crept along the hedge until he came to the drystone wall separating the small front garden from the field. He opened the gate noiselessly and made his way across an overgrown flowerbed to the lighted window. He peeped through the crack in the curtains, leaning forward over the deep sill. The first thing he saw was a dog, but fortunately it was asleep, head on paws, its body lying sideways on the worn rag rug in front of the kitchen fire. The farmer was sitting in an upright, slat-back armchair, spectacles on his nose, booted feet on the rusty fender reading a large, black-bound Bible. Septimus glanced round the rest of the low-ceilinged room. The back door was nearly opposite the window; to the right there was a wooden partition separating kitchen from parlour. Septimus guessed that the front door to his right would lead into a wooden box of a hall with the stairs going straight up. It was that hall he wanted to have a look in . . . but how? As if to underline the difficulty, he moved an incautious foot and a twig cracked. The dog did not move, but Septimus saw one ear twitch. He turned away from the window and crept across the overgrown garden. Once back in the shelter of the field hedge he crouched down, considering his position. How was he to deal with the dog?

His train of thought was disturbed by the drone of an aircraft. The noise was approaching, rapidly growing louder. It must be heading for Maydown, which was surprising since there had been no flying during the day—perhaps it was an RAF plane that had gone astray. The aircraft was close now, low and loud in the darkness, and he searched the clouds for it. The farm door opened and Septimus could see the farmer outlined in the dimly lit doorway. The aircraft landing lights flashed on almost directly above his head; the horses in the paddock whinnied at the roar of the engine, and Septimus saw the outlined shape of the aircraft close above him: the batlike, antiquated silhouette of a Swordfish against the opalescence of the cloud-obscured moon. The engine noise dwindled, rose to a brief roar, then faded to a distant mutter.

Septimus waited until the farmer went back into the house, his mind busy as he waited. Why should a man who lived in an area where planes were endlessly flying round practising deck landings leave his Bible on a Sunday night and come to his front door to watch a late-flying Swordfish? He must be used to the drone and roar of aircraft by now. And why should Rory McLusky be in such a hurry to return from Malvern? Septimus could not prove that the Swordfish was 'Gertie', but he had no doubt whatsoever that it had been.

As these speculations had been going through his mind, Septimus had been working his way stealthily round the outside of the farm buildings in order to get to the yard at the back. Now he stood in the darkness leaning on the yard gate, considering what he was going to do, prudently working out his line of retreat. Once he was in the yard he would be naked to discovery if the farmer chanced to come to the door. He had no doubt of his ability to evade the farmer in the dark, but what about the dog? He would have to chance that: there was nothing else for it.

'Here goes,' he said to himself, and softly lifted the latch of the gate. He stole across the yard, his eyes on the kitchen door and the curtained window. Hens clucked sleepily in one of the outhouses and a pig grunted, dreaming of swill buckets fathoms deep. A cat watched him from the shadows with predatory green eyes as he came to the paddock gate and opened it wide.

Where were the horses and donkeys?

Fortunately the paddock was not large and he found the five animals standing together under a tree in the hedgerow. He had some difficulty getting them to move since he did not dare to make much noise, but eventually succeeded by slapping the rump of the black horse until his hand tingled.

Once the horse started to move reluctantly down the hedgerow the other animals followed, with Septimus bringing up the rear and administering occasional slaps of encouragement.

The animals reached the gate, paused for a moment, then, urged on by Septimus, surged into the yard, hooves clattering on muddy brick, beginning to whinny and mill around at the unfamiliarity of being all together in the yard in the dark. Septimus gave a final shove to the last donkey in the procession and pulled its tail hard. It brayed in outraged protest, kicked at him and missed, but startled the others with the noise it made. Septimus slipped round the corner of the house, and as he moved he saw the black horse set off through the opposite gate and up the lane to the drovers' track.

Sheltering under the shadow of the house Septimus heard the back door open and the farmer emitting a string of most unbiblical oaths. He slipped round to the front and took a peep through the gap in the curtains into the kitchen. As he expected, the dog had gone to the door with his master. He moved swiftly to the front door, taking his pencil torch from his pocket. The door was unlocked. He opened it softly and stepped inside, leaving the door ajar behind him. Inside it was as he had expected.

The narrow white beam of his torch showed uncarpeted stairs in front, a door on either side and a jumble of coats and raincoats on pegs, wellingtons tumbled beneath them.

Swiftly he sorted through the outdoor clothing, listening to the noises from the yard. He found what he was looking for: a grey raincoat with epaulettes—and there was the small triangular tear that he had seen on the shoulder of the unknown man in the Red Cow in Killegaran. He turned off his torch and stood listening. There was no sound of stamping from the yard now, and the shouting was more distant. He ran softly up the stairs and looked out of the landing window. The yard was empty. There was a bedroom on either side of the landing. He went into the one on the left and swept the beam of the torch around. The room was sparsely furnished, but the clothes lying about the place and the bed with the blankets roughly pulled back proclaimed it as the farmer's room. The other one was clearly a spare room. It had a single iron bedstead and little other furniture: a chair, a chest of drawers, and a big, old-fashioned wardrobe. He opened the wardrobe and found it surprisingly full. There were tweed suits, jackets and trousers, all of differing styles and sizes. It was more like the stock of a second-hand clothes shop than a farm wardrobe.

The contents of the chest of drawers were much the same: a wide selection of shirts, sweaters, scarves and similar items. He grinned. Perhaps the tenant of Perrins looked after the jumble for one of the local chapels? Perhaps he was a deacon? Though that was hardly likely if his language was anything to go by.

There was the noise of a horse in the yard. The farmer was returning with his runaways, and if he had any sense he would be wondering why his gates were open, and taking a look round his property. Swiftly Septimus descended the stairs and went out into the garden, closing the door gently behind him and setting off up the hedgerow.

On his way to breakfast the next morning, Septimus met up with Rory McLusky. The Commander came looming out of the mist which shrouded the airfield, his gaberdine raincoat beaded with pearls of moisture, the dog Piddle running in lunatic circles around him. Septimus stooped to tickle the dog which promptly lay down on its back, paws waving in the air.

'Hullo, Rory. I guessed it was you who came in last night. Couldn't stand the pace of Malvern night life?'

'No,' said Rory. 'There's an affiliation order out against Pat Samuels, so we thought we'd better escape.' Then more seriously he added, 'I wanted to get the latest wizard's box back here as soon as possible. There's an exercise scheduled for Wednesday.' He grinned. 'I see you've been chasing the "Human Hairpin" around. Armed guards on the radio workshop! What next? A machine-gun tower by the Wren-nery?'

They left the dog in the vestibule and went in to breakfast together. McLusky tried to draw Septimus out as to what he had been doing during the last twenty-four hours, but Septimus was politely evasive—a tactic at which he was expert.

'I gather you took my advice and went for a walk with Pamela Byrnes. Circuit of the airfield?'

'No. As a matter of fact, I plan to do that this afternoon.'

'Come with you if you like,' said the Commander. 'I'm not flying and there's a rabbit warren up behind the rifle range. Piddle enjoys it. So do I, come to that—take a twelve-bore with me.' A sudden thought struck him: 'Tell you what. Pat Samuels has a gun. Borrow it for you if you like.'

During the morning Septimus went to the control tower and spent an hour poring over large-scale maps of the area. He noted how the road swung around the airfield, and that Perrins was hidden in a valley which was cut off from the flat land by a spur of the mountains. He located the RAF beacon where he and Pamela had drunk tea, and traced the drovers' track over the hills to Killegaran from where it started on the public road near the barn. The public road was not a very important one and he wondered if it would run to a customs post. Having committed the terrain to memory, he went up on to the flat roof of the tower to think. The anti-submarine squadron were practising their eternal 'circuits and bumps', droning round and round in circles like a children's game. It was a fine morning now, the mist banished by the sun, and he could see the glint of the Londonderry dockyard cranes, and beyond them the shimmer of the sea. To his right there were more aircraft. That would be the neighbouring airfield, RNAS Eglinton. In fact the sky seemed to be full of aircraft all preparing for the grim war at sea: U-boats and boredom; fear and death by fire or drowning—the one battle which, if lost, would drag Britain down to certain destruction.

From his high position on the roof of the control tower the airfield huts looked as insignificant as chicken coops. He identified the coop which was the radio workshop, a toy soldier in a blue uniform marching up and down, his match-stick of a rifle at the slope. And inside—since McLusky's return from Malvern—was one of the O4 sets which could make all the difference for the convoys, and it was his job to make sure its secrets did not fall into enemy hands.

Leaning on the rail, watching the Swordfish land and take off, he reviewed what he had so far unearthed. Information had been sent from Fieldman at Malvern to Shelagh Hurst at the Royal George—which was evidently a clearing house. He had not yet established any connection between the Royal George and Maydown—though he had between the Royal George and the dockyard. At Maydown the information about H2S had probably been obtained from the radio work-shop in the way he had done it himself. It would then be passed to Perrins and carried over the border to Killegaran, and from there to the German Embassy in Dublin. But who was the agent in Maydown? Rory McLusky? The dog cer-tainly seemed to know the farmer, but that was very flimsy evidence to go on, particularly since the dog was so zany. Anyway, living on an airfield, the dog had to get on with literally hundreds of people. It did a regular cadger's round of the various messes and went foraging in the kitchens or the

NAAFI canteen. What was one farmer more or less to such a gregarious beast? If not Rory, then who? There were hundreds of possibilities—though that was not strictly true. Most of the station personnel were really too young, and nineteen-year-olds did not set up 'underground' railways to Dublin. His best bet was to keep his eye firmly on the bait of O4 and hope that the spy would come to him.

As he was thinking he watched a naval truck come through the gate and draw up close to the NAAFI tea wagon standing by the open doors of one of the hangars, a crowd of ratings round the let-down counter at the side. The truck driver walked across to the tea van. Septimus frowned. Was there not something familiar about the civilian driver, distant and foreshortened as he was? He went down to the control room and borrowed a pair of binoculars. It took some moments to isolate the man in the crowd round the wagon, but then he moved away, an enamel mug in his hand. It was Tweedledum— the second of the two men who had attacked Septimus. There then was the link with the Royal George.

The man went back to his lorry and drove into the cavernous interior of the hangar. Septimus waited until he re-emerged and the truck had left the station, then he walked down to the hangar. It was noisy, echoing like a railway station, cluttered with aircraft in various stages of dismemberment. He picked his way through the seeming disorder to the office—an aircraft crate standing on steel stilts, with loft ladder, door and windows added.

The aircraft nearest the steps was McLusky's 'Gertie' and the Commander was beside it deep in conversation with a chief petty officer. He did not notice Septimus.

Peter Swann, clad in a clean brown boiler suit and a very greasy cap, was sitting at the desk in front of a window which commanded a wide, aerial view of all the varied activity in the hangar. He was consulting a technical manual.

· His greeting was friendly and he answered Septimus's questions readily enough. The only civilian drivers actually employed on the station were crane drivers. The three-ton truck which had just called belonged to the dockyard and had been bringing a crated Pegasus and various spares. Yes, a truck did come most days—and usually the same one—because spares came by sea from the main naval stores at Perth. It was practically always the same driver because it made obvious sense to have someone who knew his way round the airfield. At this point further conversation became impossible as someone started to run up an engine at full boost, setting the hangar walls rattling. The office was like the inside of some vast, unmusical instrument, the sheer noise like a physical assault. Septimus mouthed his thanks and fled from the pandemonium.

'Are you proposing to walk all the way round? It's seven miles if it's a sausage.' Septimus considered Rory McLusky's question. He had two things he wanted to do: to look at the stretch of fence nearest Perrins, and to find out all he could about McLusky.

'No,' he said, 'I'll do it in two bits. Save some for another day.' They agreed to go as far as the rabbit warren and then come back across the airfield.

It was a pleasant afternoon for a walk—much like the previous day, with spring sunshine and a sky dappled white and blue. They strode along just inside the wire, each with a shotgun under his arm, the dog sniffing in circles and occasionally cocking his leg at the concrete posts supporting the wire.

Septimus steered the conversation to Rory McLusky's early life via his flying experience. In sum he learned little more than Peter Swann had already told him, except that Rory was not an Ulsterman as Peter had said, but originally came from Dublin. He talked of flying all over the world: the Royal Naval Air Service in the First World War and the problems of attacking Zeppelins; carrying supplies to the goldfields in Alaska; mail in Australia, and what it was like to be a barnstorming pilot with an American flying circus. He had left

Ireland after the war and had never returned. Septimus could see nothing more to him than a pleasant companion and a brave man whose life had been totally dedicated to flying.

'Why did you come and join up when the war broke out?' he asked. 'After all, it isn't your war.'

Rory smiled, creasing the scar on his face. 'The Irish love a fight,' he said. 'Remember the story about the Paddy going over the top in 1915 and shouting "Bugger Cromwell" as he charged the Germans?'

There was a sudden burst of machine-gun fire from the range which they were approaching, and Septimus could see the red warning flag in the corner of the butts.

'The bunnies are at the back of the range,' McLusky said, 'but I doubt if we shall see much of them with that racket going on.'

They passed the end of the runway and in a few hundred yards the ground became hillocky with coarse grass and patches of sand. Septimus guessed it had probably once been a coastal sand dune, since they were at sea level.

McLusky put Piddle on the lead and they both loaded their shotguns, moving slowly now looking for the rabbits whose burrows were everywhere. The noise of firing continued to their right, muffled now by the rise of the dunes which protected them from the range. They came to a steep hillock and crawled up it, leaving Piddle tied to the perimeter fence. They peeped cautiously over the top. There were rabbits in plenty and they fired almost in unison. The rabbit population vanished as in a conjuring trick leaving two of their members dead on the sand. They picked up the corpses, released Piddle and strolled on.

Septimus pointed at the wire. 'Fat lot of good that is,' he said. The ground was so soft and broken up that it would have been quite easy to crawl underneath.

As he spoke there was a whine like a hornet past his ear and a sudden spurt of sand from the dune. Even as the sound of the shot reached them, both men flung themselves flat and wriggled under cover. More shots slammed over their heads as McLusky crawled one way and Septimus the other. As Septimus peered carefully through a fringe of marram grass, searching the tumbled dunes beyond the wire, he heard the double crack of McLusky's gun, and the Commander shouted, 'Up there by the two pine trees!'

Septimus could see nothing, and called back to McLusky, 'We'd better work our way round to the trench at the back of the butts.' He heard McLusky crawling toward him, cursing the dog as he crawled, for Piddle seemed to think this was some splendid game invented for his particular amusement and was putting his head on his paws and barking in Rory's face. There were no further shots, but neither of them felt inclined to find out whether the gunman was still there by standing up.

So, after a quarter of an hour, and much to the surprise of the ratings working the targets, they stood panting and brushing sand from their uniforms in the deep butts trench with 'friendly' bullets whizzing safe and high over their heads.

'Someone doesn't like you,' said McLusky, wiping sand from his shotgun.

Septimus did not reply directly. 'You got a shot at him,' he said.

'Only a gesture, my son. I thought I saw rifle smoke. But the shotgun wouldn't even have carried the distance.'

Septimus was silent. 'I go for a walk with the Commander,' he thought, 'and we both get shot at. So, of course, it can't possibly be the Commander doing the shooting.' But then who else had known about the walk around the perimeter fence? Presumably there were others in the spy ring who could handle a rifle: the Perrins farmer perhaps, or the land-lord of the Royal George. And anyway, were they trying to frighten him, confuse him, or kill him? Was it just his fancy—the self-concern of someone being shot at—or had those bullets been aimed at him rather than the Commander?

They stayed in the trench until practice ceased for the afternoon and then went home with the range party. As McLusky said, there was safety in numbers.

10

Attempted Murder

Septimus drove along the perimeter track into the gathering twilight. He was dressed in the civilian clothing he had borrowed from the dockyard, and had made certain subtle changes to his face so that superficially he looked a burly, scruffy dockyard worker. It was nothing so melodramatic as make-up: just a darkening of his hair, a greying at the temples, and an application of grime to the face and hands with particular attention to the finger-nails. He was on his way to the Royal George, but first he wanted another look at the afternoon's battleground behind the range, without either Rory McLusky for company or an indifferent marksman concealed beyond the wire. Indifferent? . . . or deliberately missing? That first shot when he was standing still should not have missed. He was, as they say, 'a sitting duck'.

He left his van on the perimeter track and walked down the deep butts trench, silent now, but echoing with the hollow thud of his heavy boots on the duckboards. As he expected, there was a faint track from the far end of the trench. It went twisting through the sandy dunes, keeping to the hollows, and it led to the boundary where the fence made an angle and the wire was fixed to a more substantial and buttressed concrete post. The strands of barbed wire were about nine inches apart, and each ended in a turn-buckle hooked to an eye in the corner post. The purpose of the turn-buckle was, of course, to tighten the wire; and indeed, most of the strands were so tight that they sang like the strings of a musical instrument when he tugged at them. But not the bottom two. They were just tight enough not to sag, and the hooks on the turn-buckles had been partially straightened so that they slid easily out of the eye. He unhooked them both and without difficulty passed under the wire. He stood a moment gazing out over the sand dunes, colourless now in the fading light. A track under the wire which no doubt led to Perrins. Was it the farmer who had been taking pot shots at him? But the farmer had no means of knowing that he would be walking the wire that afternoon. Unless . . .? He sighed softly as alternative possibilities began to take shape in his mind. It was like assembling two jigsaw puzzles with all the pieces jumbled together in one box: you did not know which piece belonged to which picture. Once again he was aware of his distaste for counter-espionage work, his longing for the decencies of 'honest' crime. He went back under the wire, replaced the strands and returned to his van.

The bar of the Royal George was crowded. Septimus, conscious of the flimsiness of his disguise, had hoped it would be. He bought a pint of bitter and found a corner from which he could watch the customers: sailors from the convoy escorts in the harbour; dockyard workers dressed like himself; slightly better dressed men who were probably clerks; a sprinkling of women.

As the evening wore on the bar became steadily more crowded, and although there was nothing that could be said to have a clear bearing on the investigation, several things became apparent. To Septimus's trained eye, the Royal George was obviously the centre of a good deal of illegal activity and would certainly be a marked pub in the books of the local 'nick'. The passing of betting slips was quite obvious, and at one table two men, a plain clothes policeman and a copper's nark, were deep in conversation. At the table next to Septimus was a very young seaman who had had far too much to drink, and was trying to impress a painted lady whose profession was blatantly obvious. And despite the poster on the wall which showed Hitler listening to a telephone conversation and proclaimed 'Careless Talk Costs Lives', an astute and sober listener would have been able to pick up a good deal of classified information from the naval personnel. In the lulls in the raucous conversation, through the billowing blue tobacco smoke, Septimus picked up a good deal about the last homebound convoy, including the name of the tanker that had been sunk. He also learned that a certain escort group was due to sail on the following day, rendezvousing with a westbound convoy in the afternoon.

He smiled sourly and bought another pint of the poor beer. Something would clearly have to be done about the Royal George, but that was not his direct concern. The most interesting thing about the pub was the telephone behind the bar. It rang quite frequently, and when the landlord came to use it he had to turn his back on his noisy customers and cup his hand round the mouthpiece. It was, Septimus reflected, an effective form of security, as good as a scrambler any day.

He was jerked out of his private speculations by a sudden and menacing change in the nature of the noise. From long experience he knew what it meant before he identified the source. There was going to be trouble.

There was a big stoker shouting angrily at a dockyard worker who was giving as good as he got. 'Bloody dockies!' shouted the stoker, his drunken face red, his brow sweating. 'When we got in the boat some bastard had pinched the rations from the bloody locker . . .'

Friends on both sides of the quarrel were trying to restrain the two men, but Septimus's practised eye told him that in about ten seconds flat fists would start flying. It was no place for him. He looked round for a way of escape. Even as he realized the impossibility of shoving his way to the bar door, the fight started with the suddenness of a summer storm. Without hesitation he lifted the flap of the counter, walked behind the bar and through the door leading to the back premises. He moved so swiftly, and the barmaid was so taken up with shrieking at the customers, that she did not see him at all. He went down the corridor to the door which opened on to the yard. It was locked and bolted from the inside. As he opened it, he heard footsteps clattering on the uncarpeted stairs—no doubt the landlord on his way down to the bar.

Quickly Septimus left the door and stepped back into the office. He went across to the window from which he had escaped before, and was about to open the curtains when he suddenly paused. There was something odd about the room, something familiar, yet different from the last time he had been in it. He wrinkled his nose. That was it! A smell which he had last noticed during the afternoon—cordite, very faint but distinct. He went back to the door and eased it open. The roar of the fight and the sound of breaking glass came from the bar. The bar door suddenly swung open and a chair came hurtling down the corridor.

Clearly, the landlord had his hands full, but it would not be long before the police arrived. He closed the office door and switched on the light. It did not take him long to find the source of the smell. It came from the wastepaper basket under the desk. There was a piece of oily rag about four inches by two. It was stained with soot and oil, and Septimus recognized it immediately. It was a 'pull through', a piece of cloth which had been used for cleaning the barrel of a rifle after it had been fired.

He switched off the light and climbed out of the window. A minute later he was strolling away from the Royal George; and he watched with a certain glee as a police car sped past him and a naval patrol came round the corner at the double, their studded boots striking sparks from the cobbles.

As Septimus walked into the officers' quarters Pamela Byrnes came down the corridor to greet him.

'Hullo,' he said, surprised, 'I thought you were supposed to be locked in the Wrennery by now.'

'Yes, I am,' she replied, 'and there'll be terrible trouble if they find out. But—Septimus—it's important.'

'Well . . .what?'

'You know you said I was to tell you if there was anything different about your cabin?'

'Yes.'

'Well. I brought one of your clean uniforms across after supper—and that's when I noticed. Someone's been fiddling with the bed. I left your pyjamas on top of the turned-down sheet, but someone's tucked them half under the pillow.'

'It couldn't have been one of the other stewards?'

She shook her head. 'No. We all have our own cabins, and I remember exactly how I left the bed this morning.'

Septimus considered, the rifle shots of the afternoon fresh in his mind. He thanked Pamela and sent her back to her quarters, promising to do his best to sort out any trouble.

She smiled at him. 'I'll not get caught. There are ways into the Wrennery. You'd be surprised.'

He smiled back. 'What a dissolute lot you are.' He saw her safely out of the block and went back to his cabin.

Apart from the bed, nothing looked different; and observant though he was, he acknowledged, with a warm stab of gratitude to Pamela, that he certainly would not have noticed anything different about his pyjamas.

He inspected the room carefully, but there was nothing else to raise suspicion. He stood at the foot of the bed and considered the smooth, grey blankets, the white oblong of folded sheet, and his blue pyjamas half under the pillow. 'Apple-pie beds,' he thought, 'like little boys in prep schools. Only they might go off bang.'

Without Pamela's warning he would simply have pulled those pyjamas out from under the pillow. What nastiness would follow? Or maybe the nastiness was in the bed itself, the pyjamas a mere lapse of memory on the part of the practical joker.

He looked first at the underside of the bed. There was nothing to see but a diamond mesh of springs and the striped cover of the mattress. He ran his hands lightly over the top blanket, feeling for anything that had been placed in the bed. There was not so much as a wrinkle. Starting at one side by the pillow, and with such caution that he hardly caused the mattress to tremble, he untucked everything, working his way down the side, across the bottom and back to the pillow on the other side. Next, he went to the foot of the bed and cautiously slid the blankets off one by one, until the two sheets remained. He removed the top sheet and still there was nothing, just the smooth snowscape of the bottom sheet and the blue pyjamas sticking out from beneath the rounded iceberg of pillow. Whatever it was was under the pillow, not in the bed.

He sat down and lit his pipe, considering the various possibilities. He could think of various nasty surprises you could hide under people's pillows, but they were mostly fairly sophisticated devices. He doubted if they would exist in the armoury of a Maydown spy, and there had been little time to obtain anything from Dublin. No, it was going to be crude. Crude but nasty.

He laid down his pipe and went and knelt by the bed as if he was about to say his prayers. The incongruous thought crossed his mind, so he mentally commended himself into the hands of God and slowly inserted a hand under the pillow. His little finger encountered something hard. His hand went rigid, so that he had to relax by an act of will. He wiped the sweat from his eyes with his disengaged hand, then explored the object with fingertips soft as butterfly's wings. It was cold . . . it was made of metal . . . it was ridged in diamonds like a pineapple . . . it was round—no, it was oval . . . like an egg . . . bigger than an egg. His breath hissed between clenched teeth. It was a hand-grenade, and in a way, it was worse to know what it was, because he had too much knowledge and he knew that if he made a mistake now it would surely blow his head off.

Inch by creeping inch he slid his fingers round the thing until he could feel the smoothness of the spring handle—the firing lever which would fly up at right angles to the body of the grenade, start the fuse and detonate the contraption. He passed his hand firmly over the lever to hold it in position, and felt with his index finger for the safety pin. There was no safety pin. The lever must be held down in some other way. Against the palm he could feel a strip of cloth, the metal of the grenade cold on either side of it. Evidently the lever was tied down. With a relaxation of tension that was like the sudden deflation of a balloon, he realized how the trap was intended to work. His hand closed firmly round the grenade and he drew it gently from beneath the pillow.

The device was simple, neat and deadly. The cord of his pyjamas had been knotted round the grenade so that the firing lever was held in place when the safety pin was removed. Had he pulled the pyjamas from beneath the pillow the grenade would have come with them, and then—because of its weight—slipped from the loop of cord. He looked at the time scale on the fuse setting which allowed a choice between nought and ten seconds from the movement of the lever to the detonation of the bomb. It was set at one second. The explosion would have been virtually instantaneous, and but for Pamela's alertness he would now undoubtedly be dead.

With the grenade held tight he took a metal coat-hangar from the wardrobe and forced the hook through the safety-pin holes. Then he laid the thing down, got a screwdriver from his toolkit and carefully extracted the fuse. He picked up his pipe and sat down, partly to allow time for the reaction to pass, partly to fit this new piece into his two complicated puzzles.

The afternoon's business might or might not have been an

attempt on his life. He had reservations about it. It was too
. . . what was the word? Histrionic. But there was no manner
of doubt about the lethal nature of this attempt. But why?
And by whom? Because he was getting close to the truth?
Because he had to be removed for some urgent practical
reason—like the fact of the O4 set in the radio workshop?
Something to do with the experimental flight over the convoy
scheduled for Wednesday? He set himself to imagine what
would have happened had he been killed. Murder would not
necessarily have been suspected—at least not immediately.
He had given enough people on the station cause to think
him at best peculiar, at worst crazy; and people who got
blown to bits by grenades—other than in battle—usually did
it to themselves, either by suicide or by sheer stupidity. 'The
pongo was playing about with a Mills bomb,' he could hear
the young men in the wardroom saying over their pink gins
before dinner. No, such a spectacular disaster would serve
the twin purposes of getting him out of the way and focusing
all attention away from O4. Ruthless and effective—but then
war was not the proverbial vicarage tea party. He smiled at
the idiotic cliché and went to bed.

In bed he set himself to work out how he would steal the
secrets of O4 if that was his job. He reached no clear conclu-
sion—except that, if an opportunity could be found, it would
take him no longer to photograph the secrets of O4 than it
had taken him to photograph those of H2S—and that was a
very short time indeed.

He awoke at about three o'clock, struggling out of the grip
of a nightmare, knowing that he was trying to shout some
sort of warning to Pamela, that he was fighting desperately
for both their lives. He lay on his back trembling, feeling his
damp pyjamas sticking to his body. He had suffered from
nightmares in recent months and recognized them as a symp-
tom of the strain he had been living under. But this had been
a particularly gruesome one—and that was not surprising
after the business with the hand-grenade. There had been a

hand-grenade in the dream. It had been mixed up with the drovers' track, the Royal George, Rory McLusky and his Swordfish 'Gertie'. Somehow the Royal George had moved itself to the banks of the stream that he had forded on his way back from Killegaran. 'Gertie'—undamaged as is the way in dreams—had landed in the middle of the stream. He and McLusky had been sitting together in the rear cockpit guarding O4, and Pamela had come out of the Royal George with Piddle. McLusky had a ball in his hand which he was going to throw to Pamela so that she could play with the dog. But it was not a ball, it was a hand-grenade, and Septimus knew that the pin was out and that Peter Swann had set the fuse to one second. And Septimus had tried to grab the grenade from McLusky, to shout a warning before it was thrown, but he could neither move nor make a sound. At this point he had woken up.

He lay awhile, pondering the dream, seeking by facing it to draw the sting of its very real terror. It was a technique he had used before when under strain. 'There is nothing to fear but fear itself.' It worked—but not completely. There was still something troubling him about the nightmare: not the terror of it, but something he ought to have remembered, something to do with Peter Swann. Why, after all, had Swann figured in the dream? The significance of the other characters in the dream was plain enough, but why was it the engineer who set the one-second fuse on the hand-grenade? Still puzzling, he fell into a troubled sleep.

I I

Find and Strike

Septimus met Rory McLusky in the bathroom at six forty-five the following morning. He had awoken early and found himself disinclined to go back to sleep because of the nagging memory of the nightmare and the thing he should remember, but couldn't.

'You're up early, Rory,' he said.

'Early birds etc. etc.,' replied the Commander. 'As a matter of fact, I'm flying today. Trying out the wizard's new box.'

'I thought that was tomorrow,' Septimus replied.

'No secrets from our intrepid anti-espionage agent: No. They moved it forward. Gives us two days to play with the convoy. Want to come?'

Septimus lifted the razor from his half-shaved face. He was startled by the offer. But—yes. With only one O4 to bother about he would be more comfortable fossicking about the sky with it under his eye. Dammit! Why had Peter Swann figured in that dream? He was so occupied with his own thoughts that he was quite unaware that he was glaring at the Commander as if the poor man was using his toothbrush.

'I said—do you want to come?'

'Can I?'

'Sure thing. You can sit in the dickey and write down numbers for Pat. Shan't take an air gunner—the only people who will be shooting at us will be our own side.'

Septimus turned back to his shaving. 'I'd like to come,' he replied. 'I suppose we're out of range of enemy aircraft?'

McLusky was brushing his teeth vigorously, so his reply was muffled.

'Except for Condors. And if any of those ill-omened bastards turn up we belt for home at full forty miles an hour. Leave him to the RAF air cover—if any.'

'And always provided the air cover hasn't shot us down in a fit of absent-mindedness,' said Septimus.

'Quite so,' said McLusky. 'The RAF don't recognize the Stringbag as an aircraft at all. They think it's a pterodactyl.'

After a hasty breakfast, Septimus paid a quick visit to the armoury and presented an astonished petty officer armourer with one Mills bomb, one coat-hanger and one grenade fuse. 'Someone left these in my cabin in a fit of absent-mindedness. You'd better check. See if they're yours.' He was out of the door before the other man could reply.

McLusky and Samuels were waiting for him in the pilots' room. They did a piratical assault on other people's lockers and came up with an adequate, if odd, selection of flying kit. This time in Gertie he was not going to freeze—at least no more than Swordfish crews usually did.

Encased in fur-lined leather, with dinghies, parachutes and flying helmets, they waddled to the hardstanding where Gertie was waiting, surrounded by a handful of overalled technicians. Peter Swann was standing to one side and Jerry Haines was draped across the fuselage more or less upside down, his head and his hands in the cockpit, his blue-clad behind exposed to the rain that was beginning to fall from a leaden sky.

'Cloud base three thousand feet, sir,' said Swann to the Commander. 'It's about ten-tenths, so it should be just the job.'

McLusky merely grunted. Haines emerged like a surfacing

diver duck. His face was red and he grinned at the Commander. 'Just checking the aerial and power line connections, sir.'

They climbed into the cockpit and Septimus fastened his straps.

The Pegasus engine started with an elephantine cough as the cartridge jerked it into life. They waited a few moments while McLusky warmed up the engine and carried out his cockpit check. There was a leading seaman in greasy blue overalls on the wing holding up a folder which reminded Septimus of the register in a school classroom. McLusky took the proffered pencil and scribbled his signature. Septimus guessed he was signing that Gertie was fit to fly. It was a wry thought that he was also signing for the lives of the three of them. Perhaps counter-espionage did have its advantages after all. At least you were dependent on yourself and not on some unknown fitter moving things by thousandths of an inch with a spanner.

The engine roared and then fell away to a gentle rumble, the controls waggled, McLusky waved away the chocks, then they were turning, trundling cumbrously to the end of the runway. The voice from the control tower was calm but tinny to Septimus's inexperienced ears. They paused at the runway's end, the engine screamed to full power, then they were moving, the cockpit seat pressing into Septimus's back. The wheels left the tarmac and suddenly they were floating up in the softly falling rain, below them the unaccustomed view of all the huts of the camp.

Peter Swann had been wrong. The cloud cover was not complete. There were ragged gaps in the murk, and through them Septimus could see glimpses of soft green fields, hamlets, roads, and very soon the coast.

In front of Septimus in the double cockpit Pat Samuels was busy with knobs and dials on the O4 set. There was a whistle and a hiccup in Septimus's ears and he found himself listening over the intercom to a conversation between McLusky and Maydown control tower.

'Radio's on the blink, Rory.' That was Pat over the intercom.
'Always bloody well is.' That was McLusky.

At five thousand feet they came out of cloud; it was a glorious sunlit morning and they were flying above a skyscape which looked like a view of Antarctica: hills and valleys, capes and bays; all on rolling white cloud with the early sun reflecting from it in every colour of the rainbow. The compass showed their course as north-west, the air speed indicator was reading 100 knots, the wind whistled in the rigging and Septimus thought how good it was to be alive.

Pat Samuels switched on the O4 and Septimus watched as the screen glowed ghostly green and the line of the scan began to rotate like the sweep hand of a clock. Pat pointed to a scribbled line which came up and faded. 'Line of the coast,' he said—and it was indeed remarkably clear; so that after a few moments to get used to the strange nature of the map, Septimus found he could pick out details of rivers and railways, hamlets and towns; while below him from the open cockpit he could see the uninterrupted carpet of rolling cloud. O4 was an impressive device, and if it was as efficient over the convoy as it was over land, it was certainly going to make a major contribution to convoy protection.

Half an hour later Pat pointed to a series of apparently stationary dots. 'There's the convoy,' he said, and gave the range and bearing to McLusky while Septimus noted down the figures. They came down through the cloud layer, emerging to a grey and weeping day with the ships of the convoy plodding patiently westward below them. They flew round it in a wide circle, prudently out of range of trigger-happy gunners. When their presence was established, they closed one of the escorts and Pat Samuels flashed a message on the Aldis. This caused a flurry of inter-ship signalling, and during the interval an RAF Hurricane positioned itself aggressively on their tail, then flew off with a waggle of wings. They climbed back through the cloud to plot exactly the composition, course and speed of the convoy, noting the varying moves of the escorts, droning round and round while Pat called out headings, distances and estimated tonnages. This went on for an hour, then Rory's voice came over the intercom.

'What we really need is a U-boat trimmed down on the surface.'

'Get them to launch a ship's boat,' Pat suggested.

'Have to be this afternoon,' Rory replied. 'We're getting short of fuel. Let's ask 'em.' They went down through cloud and Pat did more signalling with the Aldis and got the curt reply, 'Will not stop for you or anyone.'

'Tow boat astern,' Pat suggested.

'Will do. Enjoy your lunch.'

'Same to you. *Au revoir.*'

They set course for home and as they droned south-eastward Septimus, with nothing to do but think, considered the grey box of the O4. It was odd to think of its importance— the only one in Ireland; almost the only one in existence. How would he set about stealing its secrets? It wasn't all that difficult to get out of the aircraft—four bolts and a couple of electrical connections . . . His nightmare came back to his mind. Why *had* Peter Swann figured in it?

McLusky's voice came over the intercom. 'Septimus, I'd be grateful if you would take Piddle for a walk this afternoon.'

'Can't I come with you?'

'Sorry, old man. The radio's on the blink. Haines's lot will have to fix it. Means we'll be late off and the convoy will be that much further out—and you weigh too much.'

Septimus frowned. It was logical enough but he did not want the O4 out of his sight when it was not safely locked in the radio workshop.

After lunch Septimus went up to the control tower, irritated that he was separated from the O4. Control was fairly busy. Not only were they plotting Gertie's proving flight over the convoy, but there was also a simulated attack by both Maydown and the neighbouring station, Eglinton, on

Londonderry Docks. Septimus found himself caught up in the fake attack: the calm statements of the pilots over the radio about targets and angles of attack. He acknowledged a little lift of excitement. It really was rather like a ringside seat for the Air Arm's attack on Taranto. He imagined a Swordfish dropping a non-existent torpedo on a cruiser in the unoffending dockyard, and snorted. The Rear Admiral would be furious.

At length the attack ended and the voice of the Squadron-Leader came over the loudspeaker. 'Red Leader to Maydown Control. Attack completed we are on our way home.' The controller acknowledged, pushed back his headphones, and looked at the clock.

'They should be back in forty minutes,' he said; then to the signalman sitting beside him, 'Ring the air engineer and tell him to stand by. Then ring the Captain's office and tell them.' He turned to Septimus. 'Big stuff this. They're going to refuel and re-arm and make a second strike at dusk. Eglinton as well.'

'Why forty minutes to return?' Septimus asked. 'Derry's only five minutes away.'

'Commander "F" gave them a fancy box-course to fly— three sides of a square—so that they come in over the sea.'

While the aircraft were returning Septimus went down to the wardroom for a break. When he returned later there was an unusual air of formality among the personnel in the control tower. It was explained by the presence of the small, erect figure of the Captain standing beside the Flying Commander, his hands in the regulation 'at ease' position behind his back. Both men were gazing out of the window. The Captain turned as Septimus came in. 'Ah, Treloar. Come to see the fun?'

'Yes, sir. See how the other half lives.'

The Captain smiled and turned back to the window where the squadron was already taxiing to the end of the runway, as ungainly as a family of enormous prehistoric ducklings.

The control officer looked up at the Captain. 'Do you want to hear the take off, sir?'

McLeod nodded. 'Put it on the loudspeaker. See if they chatter like a gaggle of schoolgirls.' But they didn't. From 'Red Leader, A Apple' to 'G George' they formally requested permission to take off, were granted it and rumbled off down the runway into the evening.

The Captain looked at his watch. 'Not bad,' he said. 'One minute forty seconds.'

The tension in the control room slackened as the squadron winged out to sea on the first leg of their box-course. Then one of the radio operators turned to the controller.

'Sir. I've lost contact with Commander McLusky.' There was a silence in the glass-walled room and a dozen heads turned to the speaker.

'Suddenly?' Commander 'F' put the one word into the silence.

'No, sir. They were making a routine course report, and Lieutenant Samuels was complaining about bad reception. And my reception got worse till he went off net altogether.'

'You tried the other channel?'

'Yes, sir. All I got was static.'

'Samuels was having trouble with the radio this morning, sir,' said the control officer, 'that was why they were late off this afternoon.'

'Yes, I know,' said the Commander; then to the radio operator, 'Keep trying to raise them. Use both channels.' He turned back to the Captain. 'Knowing Rory, sir, he'll probably press on, radio or no radio. The convoy will be out of range by tomorrow.'

The Captain merely grunted. The matter was for the moment closed, at least until further information came in. Attention was now focused on the 'Green' squadron who were taking off from Eglinton.

Septimus went out on to the gallery to think. There was a chill wind blowing from the west which matched the chill in his heart. Somewhere out there in the fiery sunset was the one operational O4 in charge of a mad Irishman; anything up to a hundred and fifty miles away by now, out over the grey sea. Two men, frail fabric-covered wings and a single engine— and there was nothing, absolutely nothing he could do. He went back into the warmth of the control tower to be on hand when any news came through.

Radio silence had descended on the two attacking squadrons and the Captain had departed, leaving instructions that he was to be kept informed about McLusky. Mugs of tea were being drunk and, on the surface, the atmosphere was more relaxed. But there was an underlying tension. They did not speculate as to what was happening, because speculation was futile; nor did they bother the radio operator with questions. He would report when he had anything to report. So the minutes crawled by, and from time to time they caught one another looking at the clock. It reminded Septimus of a group of guests at a boring party wishing it was time they could decently go home.

The phone rang and was answered by a Wren telegraphist. She turned in astonishment to the Flying Commander.

'Sir. It's Lieutenant Samuels.'

'Who?' The monosyllable was like the shattering of glass in the sudden stillness.

'I mean . . . it's the observer, sir . . .'

Commander 'F' grabbed the phone and the occupants of the tower listened in strained silence to one side of a conversation consisting mostly of questions and affirmation, and ending with the cryptic comment, 'You stay there, Pat. We'll send a truck for you.' The Commander put down the phone and turned to the controller. 'Their engine was cutting. McLusky ordered Samuels to bail out because of the mountains. Full emergency procedure. You—Parkins—inform all airfields. You—Jones—get on to the engineer officer. You— Overy—ring . . .'

Septimus heard no more. The kaleidoscope of his ideas

whirled, then with what seemed like an audible click they fell into a new pattern. He knew why Peter Swann had figured in his nightmare. He remembered the very words the engineer had used about McLusky. It was the morning of their arrival at Maydown, and Swann had been showing him around. 'Rory had an engine failure,' he had said, 'so he put the Stringbag down on a straight stretch of unmade road.' That was it! The Swordfish might be an obsolete aircraft, but you could land it on a matchbox. And McLusky—according to Swann—was about the best pilot in the Air Arm and had been a stunt flyer between the wars. He had closed one way to O4 with his guard on the radio workshop. They were taking another and much more dangerous way. With absolute certainty, Septimus knew what was happening. He knew where Gertie was, and O4. The activity in the control tower was such that no one was taking any notice of Septimus. No one heard him mutter aloud, 'Dear God! Septimus, you are a bloody fool.'

He ran for the stairs.

I 2

Landing Strip

Heedless of the astonishment he was causing, Septimus sprinted at top speed along the tarmac. Questions were prickling in his mind about the best action to take, but mainly about the shortage of time. Piggins would have to produce some RAF police, but there was no time to find Piggins. Pamela was in the corridor of the officers' quarters and he

unceremoniously dragged her into his cabin behind him—
much to the astonishment of a passing sub-lieutenant. He
started to undress, changing swiftly into his dark clothing,
explaining as he did so. She took it all with remarkable calm,
accepting the truth of what he was saying without argument.
Selecting equipment from his case, he said, 'So, you'll have
to find Piggins. Or if not him, go to the Captain. But I want
help up there as soon as possible. Think you can do that?'

'I'll try,' she said, 'but it'll sound a bit wild coming from a
Wren steward. What if they just think I've gone bonkers?'

'I'll scribble you a note,' he said, 'and you can have my
real identity card. That'll convince Piggins, and the Captain
knows about me, anyway.'

'I'll fix it,' she said.

'Good girl.' He ran for the door.

'Oh, and Septimus . . .' He paused and looked back.
'Septimus . . . be careful.'

There was yet sufficient light for him to drive fast along the
lonely road that led round the airfield to Perrins and the
border. He turned into the track that led to the RAF radio
site and parked his van in a field entrance, concealing it as
best he could. He moved quickly and silently down the side
of the field in the cover of an overgrown hedge. There were
cows in the field, and he kept a wary eye out, in case he
should disturb them and give away his position to any possible watcher. He forced his way through a weak place in the
hedge into the next field, skirting round Perrins at what he
hoped was a safe distance—although there was no sign of life
on the farm. So, after a couple of miles of rough country, he
came out on the broken ground where Piddle had chased the
rabbit and led Pamela and himself to Perrins.

He was moving much more cautiously now, crouching
right down, fearful of sentries, taking what cover the hillocks
and rocky outcrops provided. He stopped, lying full length in
a position to overlook the flat portion of the drovers' track.

There was nothing and no one on it—certainly not the Swordfish which he had been expecting to see. He lay on his stomach breathing heavily, his sense of conviction shattered. He had been so sure! First there had been the dog's familiarity with the Perrins farmer; then his growing suspicions of McLusky; the curious shooting incident; the much more serious hand-grenade; and finally the loss of radio contact and the convenient necessity for Samuels to bail out. He had been as certain as he had ever been of anything that McLusky had come in round the side of the mountains, landed and handed over the secrets of O4 to agents from over the border, probably by photographs. Then he could return to Maydown with some plausible story about the engine deciding to come back to life.

But there was nothing to see, and he had moved so fast that the operation could not possibly have been completed; and at that very moment Pamela was contacting Piggins and he was going to look every size and shape of a complete fool.

While these uncomfortable thoughts were going through his mind he had been lying quite motionless gazing at the empty track. He suddenly stiffened, pushing himself up on his forearms. Photographs in this half light would require a flash attachment. A hiding place! The barn? No. You could not possibly get an aircraft into the barn. Baffled, but intent now on the new possibility, he crept forward to the grassy track, feeling horribly exposed as he left the shelter of the broken ground. If there was a place of concealment, there would certainly be a sentry. Crouching down, he searched along the track until he came to a muddy patch. He had been right after all. Even with the light almost entirely gone it was possible to see the deep and broad rut of the wheel of a heavy vehicle: and it was no tractor wheel, for there was no tread pattern. It had struck him as odd that the tyres of a Swordfish were treadless.

He squatted on the track, gazing around. On one side was the broken ground, on the other open field. Down toward the road was the silhouette of the barn just visible against the night sky, while up the drovers' road there was the lowering bulk of the mountains and the narrowing valley. He turned back to the barn. Now was there, or was there not, a sudden pinpoint of light against the end of it where the doors were? It flared out for an instant, and then was gone. But he knew what it was. He had seen it on the night he had raided the radio workshop. It was a man lighting a cigarette with the match cupped in his hands.

He wriggled back into the cover of the broken ground, still puzzled as to how the aircraft could have been brought into the barn. Had they perhaps taken out the set and left the aircraft outside? The answer came as he made his way as fast as possible through the hillocks, and he nearly laughed, it was so absurdly simple. The Swordfish was a naval aircraft, there-fore its wings were designed to fold precisely for the purpose of getting it into confined spaces. It was very neat! Shielded by the mountains, McLusky could get down on the strip and taxi to the open doors. It would be a matter of seconds to fold the wings and push Gertie in. The risk of detection would really be very slight.

Septimus had worked his way through the broken ground until he was opposite the barn, and he could now see the outline of the watcher by the door, his face occasionally illu-minated by the fiery point of the cigarette. Septimus crawled on until he was opposite the back of the barn, paused a moment, and then flitted across the track. He stood, trem-bling, with his back to the stone wall, close under the over-hanging eaves, but he had not been detected. He went round the back and up the far side. It took a long time because of the brambles, nettles and accumulated rubbish by the wall and he was terrified of making a clatter. As he moved he could hear the murmur of subdued voices from inside.

He reached the final corner and paused. It was going to be very difficult to dispose of the guard silently, and even more difficult to get into the barn and cover everyone inside with his automatic. He did not know how many there were, or where they would be standing. He made up his mind, crouched down and put one eye round the corner. The watcher was scarcely six feet away, leaning back against the nearer barn door. Septimus fumbled on the ground by his feet. First he found a tin can, but rejected it as not heavy enough; then his fingers encountered a rusty length of iron— it felt like an old strap hinge, and would answer his purpose very well. Next, he took out a length of picture cord: thin and very strong, with a wooden toggle at either end. From his crouching position he lobbed the hinge round the corner, sending it in an arc high across the front of the barn. It landed with a satisfactory thump and rattle on the far side. He waited for perhaps a second, then, quickly and noiselessly hurled himself round the corner.

The guard had unpropped himself from the door and had turned toward the noise. He heard nothing of Septimus's coming. The first he knew was a knee crashing into his back and a terrible pain across his windpipe like a red hot wire. His breathing was cut off before he could make a sound, and his head and shoulders were pulled back until his neck was on the point of breaking. It was impossible to move, and there was a roaring in his ears like the sound of a waterfall. A voice spoke through the roaring.

'I'm going to slacken this cord so you can breathe. If you make the slightest sound I'll break your neck.'

Slowly Septimus slackened the pressure until he could hear the air rasping in the guard's throat. He transferred the two toggles to one hand, and keeping his knee on the man's backbone, put the muzzle of his pistol against the nape of his neck.

'This is a gun,' he said, giving a vicious prod. 'I'm going to take the cord and my knee away. If you so much as move I'll blow your head off. Raise your right arm if you understand.'

Instantly the right arm came up, and Septimus put his foot to the ground, loosened one end of the cord and slipped it into his pocket. Then, still keeping the pistol boring into the other man's neck, he yanked his arm up between his shoulder blades in the classic half-nelson. Even at that tense moment it crossed his mind that if the police had taught him the half-nelson, it was the Army who had taught him the business with the cord. He grinned savagely. Police brutality seemed almost civilized in comparison.

He prodded with the pistol. 'Move,' he whispered. 'Move —very slowly and quietly. Face against the wall.' When the man stood spreadeagled against the wall Septimus could breathe more easily. If someone came out of the barn now he would have a few seconds' grace to do something about it. Even so, he was careful to keep the savagery in his voice.

'You're going to answer some questions,' he said. 'I know the answers to some of them—so you'd better tell me the truth.' He emphasized the point with the gun muzzle.

He started his catechism.

'Where did you come from?'

'Over the border.' The answer was a croak—but there was a guttural quality about it which led Septimus to his next question.

'What nationality?'

'German.'

'How many of you came?'

'Two.' So the questioning went on. Despite the urgency of the situation and the shortage of time, Septimus simply had to get as clear a picture as he could of the situation inside the barn. It took perhaps a minute, though it seemed like a week, before he was satisfied. The two of them had come on horseback; the horses were in the field at the back of the barn; inside were McLusky, two other men, both Irish, and the second German who was examining and photographing the O4 set. 'I bet he is,' thought Septimus grimly, hoping that Pamela had managed to find the security officer and help would soon arrive. But he dare not risk waiting; he must use his slender advantage of surprise.

'Right, Fritz,' he whispered, 'this is what you're going to do. You're going to open the door, and step just inside, and you'll ask "How's it going?" You'll ask it as naturally as possible—"How's it going?" Because I shall be right behind you with this gun in your neck, and I'm longing for an excuse to blow your head off.' The German nodded and they moved slowly back round the corner to the door.

The door creaked as 'Fritz' pulled it open. Septimus flattened himself against the other door, the gun still in position. The murmured conversation inside stopped. The light streaming through the widening gap seemed very bright.

'Shut that door!' That was McLusky's voice.

'I only wanted to know how it's going.' The German, in mortal fear, was playing his part as well as he could.

Septimus put his hefty foot into the man's side, sent him crashing across the stone floor, and jumped through the gap himself. There was a split second which etched the strange scene on Septimus's memory. It was like a Rembrandt study in light and shadow: the surprising shape of the Swordfish aircraft; the group of men frozen in the moment, their faces to the door; white light from the lamps, and long fingers of shadow reaching into the dusty recesses of the barn.

He pointed the gun at the roof, and pulled the trigger. The explosion seemed large in the cavern of the barn, and there was blue gunsmoke against the light.

'Still everyone!' he shouted. 'Fritz' lay still by the wall, the group of men by the bench held their frozen poses, grouped around the O4 set: McLusky in flying kit; Tweedledum and Tweedledee; and the tall blond German whom Septimus had last seen in the Red Cow in Killegaran.

'I'll shoot the first one that tries anything—and it'll give me the greatest of pleasure. Earn me a medal, I shouldn't wonder. Slowly now . . . Hands on top of your heads . . . Slowly. Go and stand facing the wall.' He beckoned with his disengaged hand to 'Fritz'—'You too.'

It required intense concentration to watch five men at once

—even if they were moving in slow motion, and McLusky could not slide slowly from the bench to the floor with his hands on his head. He jumped, and as his heels hit the stones his right hand jerked down. Septimus fired even as the hand reached for the spanner lying on the bench. The spanner leapt up, and McLusky cried out with pain, wringing his fingers.

'Next time I'll blow your brains out,' Septimus snarled.

He heard the slightest creak of the barn door behind him and spun round. He saw the face of the Perrins farmer in the bright light before the blow with the life-preserver hit him on the side of the head and blackness overtook him.

13
Mayhem in a Barn

Septimus was looking down a long vista of what appeared to be an uneven stone landscape. There were lines like canals going in various directions. It made him think of what he had read about the canals on Mars. But he could not be on Mars. And why did both his arms move together when he tried to touch the side of his head where it was hurting so abominably?

Memory came flooding back, and he struggled to a sitting position on the stone floor, gasping with pain, sick with the fiery serpents which writhed across his retina. He leaned back against the wall. The barn was empty, lit by a single powerful electric lamp on the bench. The barn doors were closed and there were sounds of movement outside, sounds of men heaving: so the Swordfish had not yet taken off. He wondered muzzily how long he had been unconscious—probably not all that long. It did not take long to put the O4 back into the aircraft, and they had probably almost finished their work when he arrived. He blamed himself bitterly. He should not have left the barn door open behind his back—it was his business to foresee such things; to realize that there would be another guard at the far end of the improvised landing strip. Possibly Pamela would be on time. If not, the secrets of O4 were lost like those of H2S, and all the consequences of lost ships and drowned men would be his fault. God! How he hated this war and his own underhand part in it. He checked himself on the edge of the futile abyss of self-pity as his body began to recover from the blow and his head began to clear. He wasn't dead yet, and he had always been something of an intuitive optimist.

He looked down at his bound wrists, testing the tightness of the rope. There was some movement because the ropes were too thick for the job, though they were too tight to slip a hand out. Still, there was something gained—had they known their business, his hands would have been behind his back and tied to his feet: 'trussed like a chicken'. They had removed his belt—he could see it on the bench, but had they searched him thoroughly? He doubted it: haste and inexperience would make them careless.

He ran his bound hands down his leg. Yes, there it was, the comforting outline of the slim double-edged dagger which he kept there always and which had saved him on more than one occasion. He moved to take it out—but no. How was he to use it? Not with his hands, and only a monkey could use his feet. He looked round, seeking inspiration, knowing there was so little time, deliberately shutting out the fear which could so easily take charge. He forced himself to relax. He must think it out from first principles. The handle of the knife had to be held firm: a vice . . . a heavy weight . . . something in which he could jam the handle. A crack in the wall! He wriggled round so that he could see the wall. There were plenty of cracks, of all shapes and sizes, where the mortar had not filled the gaps between the rough-hewn stones. He carefully took out the razor-sharp knife and looked for a place to jam it. The task was not easy with the blade between his bound wrists and his thumbs on the hilt guard, but after several attempts he managed it at the expense of several not too serious cuts. As he was about to begin the delicate business of sawing through the ropes, the barn door creaked open. He was partly shielded from sight by the bench, so just had time to wriggle round and conceal the knife with his side. It was Rory McLusky, ungainly in his flying kit.

'I came to say goodbye, Septimus, and ask if there was anything I could do for you,' he said.

Septimus tried to sound as normal as possible, conscious all the while of the knife at his side.

'You can answer me a couple of questions,' he replied.

'Yes?'

'You photographed H2S in the radio workshop?'

'Yes,' McLusky replied, 'and I'd have done the same with O4 if you hadn't worked it out—then all this carry-on wouldn't have been necessary.'

'I suppose the Perrins farmer told you Piddle had given you away?'

'Yes. So I tried to put you off the scent by arranging the shooting.'

Septimus smiled, almost grinned. 'The landlord of the Royal George? That was a mistake, Rory. No one could have missed with a rifle—not at that range. Hence the hand-grenade, I suppose?'

'Yes. With O4 today what else could I do? And now? I'm sorry, Septimus, but I can't have you blowing my cover. I'm too valuable to my side where I am.'

'Your side?' Septimus replied. 'But you've served England in two wars.'

'Not since 1917 I haven't. The Black and Tans killed my father and my brother—a child of thirteen. Since then I've always fought the English.' There was really no reply to that, and Septimus could see the sadness and bitterness on the scarred face.

'Goodbye, Rory,' he said. 'If things had been different we might have been good friends.'

'We might at that. Goodbye, Septimus.' McLusky turned and left the barn without looking back.

Septimus lay a moment listening, feeling a great sadness. Two men caught in the savage, age-long tragedy of sister nations; pawns on the board of history. The German agents would certainly kill him if he did not escape; and if he did escape, his own people would probably shoot Rory McLusky. He set about escaping.

Despite the sharpness of the knife it was not easy to saw through the cords. If he pressed too hard the knife slipped from the crack; and it was difficult to get enough movement without the ropes slipping off the end of the knife—and every time that happened he cut himself. But he persevered, replacing the knife patiently, feeling the hot blood running over his fingers, listening to the noises outside and hoping he would be free before they came for him.

He heard the cough of the starter cartridge and the roar of the Swordfish engine. The Pegasus revved once and almost immediately the aircraft started to move, the noise rising and falling as McLusky manoeuvred. He cursed, pressed too hard, and the knife came out of the wall again. Perversely it slipped into the crack between two stone flags, and he spent several breath-stopping moments extracting it, fearful that it would jam or slide out of his reach altogether. He had just managed to get it out and was pushing it back into place when the Pegasus roared to full power and then the noise dwindled rapidly in the distance. He could imagine it tearing through the night towards a light at the far end of the grass track. The note changed to a mere drone as the Swordfish left the ground.

Working on the final strands of the rope, he wondered what the others would do. One of them—the Perrins farmer perhaps?—would be at the far end of the airstrip. Presumably the Germans would go for the horses and get over the border as fast as possible, and Tweedledum and Tweedledee would come back to deal with him.

The ropes came free. He chafed his wrists for a moment, bringing painful life back to his numbed and bleeding hands. There was the jingle of harness and the sound of hooves outside the barn.

Swiftly he replaced the knife in its sheath and was about to get up when he heard footsteps outside the door. It was too late to move. He laid the cut ropes over his wrists, holding the loose ends concealed between his drawn up knees, so that when the two men came in all they saw was a battered and bound prisoner sitting up in the corner of the barn.

They came and stood over him. 'Now,' said Tweedledum, the short, broad one, 'time to deal with you, and it'll be a pleasure. Get up!'

He lashed out with his foot at Septimus's side so that the cut ropes all but fell from his wrists.

'Better make sure those ropes are secure first,' said the other—which was what Septimus had hoped he would say. Tweedledum crouched down and stretched out a hand to the ropes. Septimus waited until he was actually touching them, then suddenly opened his knees and grabbed the outstretched hand by the wrist, pulling with all his strength and leaning sideways at the same time. Like a stone from a catapult Tweedledum shot forward, his head cracking against the wall with enough force to fracture his skull; then—as Septimus knew he would—he bounced off. Timing his movement with the rebound, and using his bent knees as a spring, Septimus thrust upward with all his strength and hurled the man bodily at his companion, sending them both rolling across the floor.

They stopped rolling. The first man was unconscious if he

was not dead, the other was struggling to his feet. Septimus waited until he was halfway up and then hit him under the chin. All his fourteen stone of bone and muscle was behind the blow so that it lifted the man from his feet and hurled him across the barn to lie unconscious across the prostrate body of his partner.

'Well, well,' Septimus murmured—but jerkily, because he was panting—'you two do like rolling about the place.' He stood, recovering his breath, considering his next move. The two Germans would soon be over the border. There was one way to stop them. It was not a method he liked, but for want of a better, he would have to use it.

He had recovered his possessions from the bench and was stooping to tie up his prisoners when he heard the sound of a vehicle. Help had arrived. Good for Pamela! He grabbed the lamp from the bench and, heedless of the blackout, ran into the night, waving the lamp and shouting.

There were four RAF policemen in the back of a sturdy personnel carrier, with Pamela sitting in the front between Piggins and the driver. Pamela saw the state he was in by the light of the lamp and let out a sharp exclamation of dismay. Septimus took no notice as he jumped on to the running board.

'You,' he said to one of the policemen in the back, 'arrest those two men in the barn.' Such was his authority that with a single glance at the Security Officer the policeman climbed down.

Septimus turned to the driver. 'Drive like hell,' he said.

'Where to, sir?' asked the man, not unreasonably.

'Straight ahead and as fast as possible.'

'Bloody hell!' muttered the driver as he let in the clutch and the carrier went swaying into the darkness, its masked headlights showing the driver nothing of the way ahead but a couple of circles of grass.

As they roared down the airstrip Septimus outlined the situation to Piggins, explaining about McLusky, the two men in the barn and the two men on the horses, the wind of their passage playing tricks with his voice.

The truck came to a skidding halt, swerving perilously across the grass. 'Can't get any further, sir,' said the driver. By the light of the electric lantern they could see the rocks which barred further progress. They had reached the point where the drovers' way narrowed and started to climb the valley into the mountains.

'Cut your engine,' said Septimus. In the sudden silence they were aware of the night; of a dog barking; of the mournful hoot of an owl somewhere in the trees; of the sigh of the wind; and very faintly from the valley ahead, the musical jingle of harness.

Swiftly Septimus issued his orders. Piggins and Pamela tried to argue, but Septimus was adamant. The sort of risks he was proposing to take were his business and no part of their job as ordinary members of the forces of the Crown. Time was short, and they accepted his decision without further question. The whole party climbed out of the carrier and Septimus slipped into the driver's seat after checking that there was a rope in the back. He watched them set off up the track at their best speed, then turned the carrier, after some difficulty with its unfamiliar gearbox, and drove back down the strip.

Doubtful as always about his motives, he wondered why he had really refused to take any of them with him. Because he had no desire to see Piggins or one of the policemen spend the rest of the war in a prison camp? Or was it personal pride—vanity? He had mucked up the job, so it was up to him to straighten it out? He smiled to himself as he decided that it was a mixture on the one hand of his unwillingness to involve amateurs in a piece of professional dirty business, and on the other of plain bloody-mindedness.

The policeman who had been left with Tweedledum and Tweedledee was waiting outside the barn. He came to attention as Septimus stopped the carrier, and reported with admirable calm that one of the prisoners was dead and the other still unconscious. 'He appears to have a broken jaw, sir,' he ended.

Septimus spent precious seconds on the business.

'Are you a real copper,' he asked, 'or just one for the duration?'

'I'm a constable in Civvy Street, sir. Ten years in the Met. Limehouse, sir.'

'We're neighbours then,' Septimus replied. 'Can you drive?'

'Yes, sir.'

Septimus handed over the keys of his own van, explained where it was hidden, and left the policeman to sort out the conflict between the security of his unconscious prisoner and his need of medical aid. No doubt the constable had faced similar problems during his ten years in Limehouse. He let in the clutch, drove down to the road, turned the carrier left on to the rough tarmac and accelerated in the direction of the border.

14
Out of the Valley

As he drove along the winding road Septimus's mind was occupied with two things: whether there was a border post, and making sure he remembered the route of the drovers' road from the Killegaran end. There probably would be a border post since it was a tarmac road. Well, he had a sturdy vehicle, and they did not know he was coming. The drovers' road started at a gate and ran between trees, climbing into the foothills and then becoming more open. There was the heath where you forked left, then it went down to the stream where he had rested. It climbed steeply among trees on the other side, getting much narrower; and so over the top and down the long valley to the landing strip and the barn. The steep climb up from the stream—that was the place—if he could get there in time. He did sums in his head about distances, the speed of the personnel carrier, and the speed of men riding horses along a rough track in the dark. He had to give it up. There were too many imponderables. He wished he knew exactly where the border ran in the mountains. It probably followed the stream, but he should have checked it accurately—though it had not seemed important when he was studying the topography.

He had been driving automatically and as fast as possible along a road that was steadily climbing. He rounded a curve and came back to the immediate present with a jerk. He switched off engine and headlights, knocked the gearbox into neutral and allowed the carrier to coast to a silent standstill.

Ahead, perhaps a third of a mile away, there was a light on a post, and a building beside it with more light spilling from an open door, and uncurtained windows. It must be a border post. The road snaked across open heath toward the light, beneath which he could see a white painted pole across the road. He started the engine, switched on the lights, and—after some difficulty—engaged the four-wheel drive of the carrier. As he approached the post a man in uniform came out of the building and stood in the middle of the road, the bright light throwing a sharp shadow of his upraised hand. There was a revolver in a holster at his hip. Septimus stopped the carrier some twenty feet from the guard and shouted round the windscreen, 'Can you help me? I'm looking for RNAS Eglinton.'

'Well, you've found the Eire border.' The Irish accent was heavy, the tone amused.

'Hell!' said Septimus. 'Can you show me where I am on the map, mate?'

The officer came forward, moving to the side of the road to pass the carrier. Septimus let in the clutch with a bang and pushed the accelerator flat on the floor. The carrier leapt forward like a stung horse. The guard shouted and jumped for the running board. Septimus fended him off, one hand flat on his face, sending him rolling into a gorse bush. The carrier was not travelling very fast when it hit the pole, but it was fast enough, and the four-wheel drive was designed for this sort of thing. It slowed, then gave what is best described as a heave—like an elephant pushing a log. There was a splintering noise from the pole and by the time the guard had picked himself out of the gorse, Septimus was away down the road with half the border pole jammed between bonnet and mudguard. There was the crack of a revolver from behind, but no one ever knew where the shot went.

Septimus was modestly pleased with his success. It was all very well for spies in stories to drive private cars flat out at obstacles—but it was likely to be bad for the radiator, and what use would a seized-up personnel carrier be five miles inside Eire? In his driving mirror he saw the guard run for the border building, revolver still in hand. No doubt he was heading for the telephone. 'Sensible man,' Septimus thought.

To the left of the road was a row of telegraph posts. He drove for perhaps a quarter of a mile, stopped and got out, leaving the engine running. There seemed to be no one following him. He got the coil of rope from the carrier and stood beside one of the posts. On one end of the rope was a heavy steel hook. He weighed it a moment in his hand, then hurled it into the darkness overhead. It came swinging back down again, nearly hitting him on the head, but with the rope securely over the invisible wires. He gathered the two strands of rope together and hauled. There was a twanging and snapping over his head, and the rope came free. As he coiled it he relished the thought of the border guard's excited report of the English invasion of Eire suddenly cut off. Perhaps he had even disrupted all communication between the two countries? He chuckled aloud at the thought of the international complications.

He drove on, trying to strike a balance between the need for haste and his fear of missing the gate at the end of the drovers' road. He need not have worried. Although there were heavy clouds, the high quarter moon was free of them, and it was easy to see the double line of hedgerow on the far side of the gate.

He turned off the road, closing the gate behind him, wondering as he climbed back into the carrier just how far he would be able to drive up the rough track even in this powerful vehicle.

He went roaring along, mostly in bottom gear, the carrier bucking and swaying in the darkness like a ship in a storm. He hit rocks, several times only the four-wheel drive saved him from bogging down, twice he had to stop to roll rocks out of the way, but the carrier was built to withstand this sort of treatment, and he drove on with the comforting knowledge that he was travelling far faster than any horse. He came out into the open where the enclosed lane ended, took the left fork and plunged down the valley side to the stream and ford, where he stopped. He was convinced that the stream marked the border between the two countries, and it would certainly be less of an international complication if he left the carrier in Northern Ireland. He launched the carrier cautiously into the water. He could feel the force of the current on the steering—as he had felt it on his legs. But he knew the stream was shallow, and the carrier went through without difficulty and crawled out on the far side like some prehistoric amphibian. He drove on for a further hundred yards, climbing steeply, to where the track narrowed among trees and the vehicle could go no further. He drove the bumper against the first trees so that the track was entirely blocked, switched off, and sat a moment, straining his ears in the sudden quiet. There was nothing but the rustle of the trees and the muted murmur of the stream. He took the electric lamp and the rope and climbed over windscreen and bonnet.

It was far darker now: not only because of the overshadowing trees, but also because the clouds had obscured the finger-nail moon. A soft rain started to fall. He found the place he was looking for scarcely a quarter of a mile above the vehicle at the point where the descending path turned a sharp corner and the trees were very close. He stopped, listening for the sound of horses. There was nothing.

By the light of the lamp he stretched the rope across the track from tree to tree, high enough to clear a horse's head but not his rider, straining it tight with all his strength. When it was in position he went on up the track and turned to look back. Try as he would, he could not see the rope in the darkness under the trees. Satisfied, he went back and found himself an ambush point beside a rocky outcrop a few feet above the path and close to the rope. He sat down, put the lamp within easy reach and re-loaded his automatic.

Now there was nothing to do but wait, he realized how tired he was and how much his various injuries ached. The side of his face, where the Perrins farmer had hit him, was one mass of jangling pain. His ribs were so tender that he wondered if one of them was broken. The palms of his hands were agonizing from the many cuts he had inflicted on himself, and by the throbbing in his shoulder he guessed that the earlier bullet wound had re-opened. It was at moments like this, moments of waiting, that he yearned for peace. Peace, not just as an end of war, not even as a cessation of fear—not as an absence of anything, but as a positive good in its own right. 'Love thy neighbour as thyself,' instead of 'Kill or be killed.'

He was a man of deep faith, and as he waited he tried to pray, but could not—not at that moment, not Septimus

Treloar who had killed two men in the last week, and was sitting there in the soft falling rain planning something which might well kill two more: two Germans, 'Huns', the enemy. Two men loyal to their own country as he was loyal to his. All he could do was whisper, 'God forgive me.'

The sound of a hoof on stone and the jingle of a bridle warned him of their approach. Pain, weariness and the struggles of faith and conscience fell away. Lamp in one hand, gun in the other, he waited.

The approaching sound grew steadily louder: the rattle of hooves, the creak of leather, the chink of metal. He saw the first rider as he turned the corner, but only as a darker shadow in the darkness under the claustrophobic trees. He did not see the first rider hit the rope; he heard the cry of the man, the whinnying of a terrified horse, and then a chaos of shouting and trampling, a whirling pandemonium of horses and men. He switched on the lamp.

Both men were down on the path, the leader under the hooves of the second horse, the other man lying still some ten feet up the track. Septimus ran to the aid of the first man, to save him from being trampled to death. Perhaps it was human instinct, perhaps it was compassion; whatever it was it was certainly a dangerous mistake to get too close to the flailing hooves of the wildly rearing horses. As Septimus stooped to drag the leader clear, the first horse set off at a slithering trot into the darkness. The second followed, leaping the kneeling Septimus, its hooves slipping on the loose surface, one iron shoe kicking sideways into Septimus's ankle.

He felt the crack as the bone broke, and he was sent rolling in agony down the path, the lamp spinning from his hand into the gorse. The pain was so great that for several minutes he was able to do nothing but lie there, groaning and sobbing, teetering on the edge of unconsciousness. The sound of the horses died away in the distance—presumably when they were stopped by the abandoned personnel carrier they forgot their troubles and, after the fashion of their kind, wandered away among the trees in search of grass. The unbroken electric lamp lay in its nest of gorse looking like a Christmas tree decoration. It cast shadows, long and weird, among the trees beneath which the three men lay sprawled: one dead, one unconscious and one writhing with pain.

Septimus began to recover—mainly because his foot and ankle started to go numb. He propped himself on one elbow which sent a shaft of pain stabbing up his leg. He felt in his pocket and was relieved to find the automatic still safe where he had thrust it when he went to the aid of the trampled man. He began to drag himself across the path to the lantern, biting his lip to prevent himself crying out. As he reached the gorse bush the second man groaned and rolled over. In his haste to reach the lamp Septimus put weight on the broken ankle and nearly fainted with the pain. However, he did manage to grab it and point both the lamp and a very shaky automatic at the German who was struggling to his feet. Evidently the man was dazed but not injured.

'You,' he said, 'keep still. I'm pointing a gun at you behind this lamp.' The man put up an arm to shield his eyes and stared into the blackness round the lamp. His hand moved toward his pocket.

'No!' Septimus shouted. 'Very foolish. I don't want to kill you. But I can see you and you can't see me.' The hand paused. Septimus struggled against nausea. He *must* think. The man had recovered quickly and was clearly dangerous.

'Sit down,' he said. Slowly the German sank to the path.

'Now, put your right hand on your head and take the gun out with your left hand . . . that's right . . . now slide it along the path to me.' The revolver came slithering and clattering over the stones.

'Now take your shoes off.' The man made no move.

'Do as you're told. And if you try to throw them at me I'll kill you.' It was in Septimus's mind that running in socks would not be easy on the rough track. When the shoes were laid on the path, Septimus made the man stand and turn his back. He ordered him to remove jacket and trousers, make a bundle of them with the shoes and roll the bundle toward the lamp. 'And don't try and throw it at me,' he said.

The bundle landed six feet away and unravelled across the path.

Septimus was so intent on doing what had to be done before unconsciousness overtook him that he was unaware of the strangeness of the scene: the man in his shirt-tails and stockinged feet on the stony path, the glare of the lamp, the long shadows and the falling rain.

'Now lie full length with your hands clasped behind your back,' he said. 'Go on . . . do it.' Slowly, unwillingly and still without speaking the man did as he was told.

When he was prostrate Septimus dragged himself painfully to the clothes and went through the pockets. What he was looking for was not there. The other man must be carrying them—and that made sense, since he had been in the lead. There was a wallet and a notebook which he took. The revolver he emptied and flung into the trees. He was near the end of his strength now, but he dragged himself to the trampled corpse of the first man. It was neither easy nor pleasant searching him—not least because Septimus had to keep half his attention on the prone figure of his prisoner. But he managed it, and at last found what he was looking for—two rolls of film, a small but sophisticated camera, and a sheaf of notes. His strength ebbing fast, he dragged himself to the side of the track. He found a reasonably dry spot under an overhanging rock and started a small fire with the papers and leaves torn from the notebook. He extracted the film from the camera, put it with the other two on to the fire, and added the remaining leaves from the notebook. Despite the blackness which was crumbling away his consciousness like the sea round a sandcastle, he felt a little glow of satisfaction. Whatever happened to him, the job was done. O4 was safe.

He turned the lamp on the prostrate German.

'You lie still,' he said, speaking with the slow and careful concentration of a very drunk man. 'There is nothing to risk your life for now. I've destroyed it all.'

'I will kill you if I can.' The German spoke for the first time.

'Haven't we had enough of killing?' Septimus replied.

The German said nothing. So they waited in the rain until Pamela and the others found them.

15

The South Downs

There was a lone destroyer coming up the English Channel. Septimus Treloar—who knew little of things nautical—judged by the length of its wake that it must be travelling at speed. From where he was sitting, high on the Sussex Downs, it looked like a toy boat, a boy's model of a grey warship speeding across a blue pond. It was a lovely morning, the sun high in a cloudless sky, and a delicious scent of thyme in the air.

It was six weeks since the business in Ireland had ended, but Septimus was still muddled about many of the details. His eyes turned from the destroyer to the brown-habited figure of Father Dennis sitting on the downland turf beside him. The battered boxer face creased into a homely smile. 'Want to talk about it, Septimus?'

Septimus shook his head. 'Just getting my ideas straight. Maybe talk later.'

The friar nodded briefly and turned to a minute examination of the tiny downland flowers. That, Septimus reflected. was why he liked the Franciscans. They understood the value of silence as a healing thing in its own right. Who was it called his wife 'my gracious silence'? Someone in Shakespeare, he fancied.

He had been very ill. The doctor in the Belfast Naval Hospital had told him bluntly that it was only his fine constitution that had enabled him to survive at all. The neglected shoulder wound and all his other injuries, combined with his wait in the soaking rain, had brought on pneumonia, so that he remembered little of what had happened after Pamela and the others had found him. Certain scenes stood out like oases in a desert of pain and delirium. He remembered the beam of a torch coming like a searchlight out of the darkness of the path, and Piggy Piggins's voice, sharp with astonishment, saying, 'Good God!'

He remembered Captain McLeod coming to see him—he supposed it must have been the following morning because there was sunlight streaming into a white painted room. He could remember the 'Mr Punch' face leaning over him, and he could remember laughing because it was a Punch and Judy show and he himself was the Policeman. It had seemed a very good joke at the time. He remembered how he had fought the roaring waves of darkness that were seeking to engulf him, because he knew that he must make a sensible report; it was important, but he could not for the life of him remember why.

Pamela had come to visit him—presumably on some steward's pretext about his kit. He had no idea what she had said. But he could remember her leaning over the bed and kissing him. It was the memory of her presence more than anything else that he had clung to. It was like the smell of apricots on a warm wall among the antiseptic hospital smells —like the scent of thyme here on the Downs.

His report to the Captain must have been reasonably lucid because by the time he was well enough to go to London to report to Sir John most of the loose ends had been tidied up. With difficulty, because of his crutch and plastered foot, he had thumped up the worn steps of the 'RE and Rail Transport Div.' Inside the office it was as if he had never been away. Miss Parsons had looked up from her typewriter and said, 'Good morning, Captain Treloar. I am glad to see you are convalescent.'

It was if he had been suffering from mumps. He had drunk coffee with Sergeant Dickinson, having moved—as usual—the pieces of some complicated weapon before he had been able to sit down. Dickinson was delighted with his favourable report on the trick suitcase.

So far as he had been able to tell through the smokescreen, Sir John was pleased with him. Rory McLusky, Tweedledee, the Perrins farmer and the landlord of the Royal George were all safely in prison awaiting trial. The German whom Septimus had last seen in his underpants was also under arrest, though what was to happen to him was a different question, as the whole business involved the violation of a neutral border and thus politics—a subject of which Septimus knew little and cared less. At this point Sir John had been inclined to be a bit tetchy, muttering about international incidents. However, he had blown down his pipe, making it erupt in a volcano of sparks and said, 'You were lucky, Septimus. The border runs along that stream, so the whole thing happened in UK territory.'

'What about the personnel carrier?' Septimus asked.

Sir John laughed outright at this. 'That Captain—whatsisname—McLeod deserves a medal. After you'd made your report to him he anticipated complications with the Eire Government, so he treated it as he would have done a crashed aircraft—sent out a recovery party before the politicians got busy. They chopped down the trees and widened the track. Brought the vehicle back that way. They brought the dead man as well. Buried him as a shot-down member of the Luftwaffe. So now all he is doing is apologizing to the Irish authorities for a drunken escapade by one of his officers, and promising compensation and the most summary disciplinary action.'

Sir John had then stood up and offered him a gin—which was very pleasant, not least because it was a gesture which marked the closing of the file. As they had chatted over the drink Sir John had said something which pleased Septimus very much.

'Oh, by the way, that friend of yours at Malvern—Burroughs. He did a first-class cover-up over that business of the clerk that fell off the roof. Saw the importance of it, and acted on his own. It was all tied up with the local police before we got on to it.'

'He's a good man, sir,' Septimus said.

'Yes. I know. I've asked him to join us.'

Septimus came back to the present. It was wonderful to sit here in the sun with Dennis. The Franciscans had suggested that he should spend at least part of his convalescent leave at St Clare, their novice house. So here he was, with Dennis for company, living in the gracious Elizabethan manor tucked in a fold of the Downs above the peaceful village of Bramble.

He glanced at the friar. Dennis was sitting with his knees drawn up, very still, his hands clasped round his legs, looking at a rabbit. The rabbit was also sitting up, looking at Dennis, equally still. It was both comic and curiously moving. The friar's habit was brown, as was the rabbit's fur; so that despite the long ears of the one and the battered boxer's ears of the other, they looked as if they were related—much as a Great Dane is related to a Yorkshire terrier. Septimus chuckled, thinking that St Francis would have appreciated the scene. The rabbit shot away and disappeared with a flourish of its powder-puff tail. Dennis came across the close-cropped turf and looked down at Septimus for a long moment.

'Well,' he said, 'is it over, Septimus?'

Septimus sighed deeply. 'Yes. It's over.'

' "I have not found so great faith. No, not in Israel." '
Dennis quoted the words from the Gospel softly.

Septimus was puzzled. 'What do you mean?'

'Just what the Lord said to the captain who wanted his
servant healed. Didn't criticize the man for doing his job.'

Septimus grunted. 'Sort of biblical scholarship I might
expect from an ex-prizefighter.' But he was obscurely com-
forted nonetheless. He hauled himself to his feet and stood,
leaning on his stick. They moved off along the path which
led down to Bramble.

There was a dark-haired girl coming towards them wearing
a dress the colour of ripe oats, swinging along with the free
stride of someone who loved the great hills. Septimus stopped
in his halting progress. It was Pamela. Her pace slowed as she
came toward them and she stopped about six feet away.

'Hullo,' she said doubtfully, the corners of her wide mouth
drooping.

Septimus was wearing corduroy trousers and an old tweed
jacket which the Franciscans had found for him. She had not
expected to see him out of uniform, and it puzzled her a little.
For his part he could say nothing because she looked so beautiful. So they stared at one another, unaware of the friar.

'I've got a fortnight's leave,' she said hesitantly. 'I came
down to see how you were.' Tardily Septimus remembered
his manners and introduced Dennis.

The friar said, 'I've got to get down to St Clare for Sext.
Lunch at one—if you're coming, Septimus.' He smiled at
Pamela and strode away along the path.

'Have you just come for the day?' Septimus asked.

She blushed. 'I didn't know, Septimus. I brought a bag. I
left it at the Bluebell in the village.'

He limped towards her and took her hand. 'Come on,' he
said, 'let's go and book you in.'